DAVID POLLARD

THE ALIENATION OF LUDOVIC WEISS

This is for Alexandria
My best friend and constant support

BY THE SAME AUTHOR

ALSO PUBLISHED BY AMAZON

SHORT STORY COLLECTIONS

His Cat and Other Strange Tales (Coming March 2020)

PLAYS PUBLISHED BY LAZYBEE SCRIPTS
(www.lazybee.com)

Can Malone Die?
Aspects of a Betrayal
Clause Fourteen
Illusion/Delusion

MONDAY

Cancer starts unobtrusively and with no fanfare. A rogue cell divides and divides again. A spot of blood appears where it is not expected. In just such a way the settled and comfortable life of Ludovic Weiss began to disintegrate.

Nobody likes Monday morning and Weiss was no exception. It was not that he found his employment particularly onerous. In fact he relished his position within the Compliance Department. He enjoyed the status it afforded him heartily. He valued the companionship of his work colleagues and he felt assured that his superiors held him in high regard. His workplace was like an extension to his home and his family.

No-one, however, wants to leave behind the pleasure and leisure of the weekend and embark on another week of attention to detail, meetings that have to be attended and ever present deadlines. This particular weekend had been especially pleasurable. The weather had been dry and autumnal with just a hint of the chill that presages winter.

On Saturday Weiss had shopped with his wife. After, they had lunched and then gone to the cinema. They were showing a double bill of American films noirs. It was a genre with a strong appeal for Weiss. He liked the use of black and white film and found the inevitability of a disastrous ending for the main protagonists oddly satisfying, almost cathartic. Lil remarked wryly, as she always did, that this simply showed the darker side of Weiss' soul.

On Sunday morning they had made love as usual. Afterwards Weiss lay beside Lil enjoying her warmth and her soft woman smells. Weiss made breakfast and they sat together leafing through the Sunday newspapers. Later they drove into the country and went to lunch with Lil's parents.

Weiss liked his in-laws and looked forward to the weekly visits. This was not least because he felt sure that both mother and father respected and liked him in their turn. They showed him the due deference that came with his rise within the Department. In one memorable moment, when a considerable amount of wine had flowed, Lil's father had actually complimented Weiss on his ability to acquire both money and status. In short Lil's parents saw Weiss as the good provider they had always wanted for their only daughter.

Lil's parents occupied a house outside the city. It was pleasant to drive out there among the trees now covered in the russets and yellows of autumn. It was still warm enough, at the height of the day to sit in the garden with their pre-lunch drinks.

Lil's father was in fact a liberal host and the wine flowed throughout the afternoon. Lil's mother provided an excellent lunch and Weiss enjoyed a relaxed afternoon with his family.

As they drove home Weiss and Lil talked about their plans for a summer vacation trip. Weiss wanted to go to the lakes as usual. Lil was holding out for something a little more adventurous. By the time they had arrived home Weiss had all but given in to Lil and told her to get some information so they could make their bookings. Later that evening Ludovic and Lil lingered over a final glass before retiring to peaceful sleep.

By contrast this Monday morning dawned overcast and a chilly drizzle persisted throughout the morning.

No city on earth, however well regulated, has managed to arrange for the morning commute to be free of stress and delay. The tram lines in the centre of Weiss' city were under repair and the traffic crawled past the work site churning up a slurry of yellow brown mud. Joylessly Weiss joined the queue of cars that stop-started on its way into the city.

The Compliance Department occupied an office block in the central business district of the city. It was a landmark in its own right, rising several stark grey stories above the surrounding buildings and in the centre of an extensive tarmac area devoted to car parking for the Department's officials. The whole campus was protected by a high wire fence which was topped with razor wire.

Weiss turned into the campus, passing through the guarded entrance gates that swung open for him at the sight of the small, square blue badge attached to his windscreen. He gestured thanks to the guard in his booth who returned the greeting with a deferential salute.

The residue of Weiss' good humour, which he had managed to retain despite the traffic delays, ebbed away as he approached his parking space. Someone had already parked there.

Weiss drew up behind the trespasser and switched off his engine. The car in his space was new and shiny and unmarked by any sign that it had been driven through the muddy streets. Weiss ran his hand along its lustrous dark green paintwork. He was seething inwardly as he looked about in a vain attempt to spy out the owner.

There was no point in wreaking damage on the interloper although for a passing moment Weiss contemplated letting down a tyre or ripping off a colour coordinated windscreen wiper. The drizzling rain was finding its way under his collar, cooling his ire. This would have to be sorted out calmly and the culprit reprimanded coolly with sharply pointed and well considered words. Weiss got back into his car and drove out of the compound.

After circling the Compliance Department building and the surrounding streets for what seemed like an age Weiss found a parking space several blocks and some minutes soaking walk from the Department building. He trudged back to his office. The rain continued to fall steadily and soaking as only chill drizzle can. When he finally reached his office his weekend mood had completely evaporated.

Else seemed to take a much too relaxed view of the incident for Weiss' liking. She would take care of it, she soothed. There had been a number of new starters at the Department. It was probably all a mistake on the part of one of the new people who hadn't been properly inducted into the Department's protocols.

How, Weiss asked, was it possible for even the most uninformed individual to make such a mistake. The fact of his entitlement, his exclusive entitlement, to that parking space was clearly indicated. There was an enamelled sign designating the spot as his own and pointing out his entitlement as a consequence of his rank. Only a blind man or someone of a defiant persuasion would thus usurp his position.

Privately, and he would never speak about this suspicion aloud, he wondered if this was some conspiracy to vex him. He speculated on the identity of the culprit. He asked himself who he had offended recently.

His jacket was still soaked from the drizzling rain. Else took it from him and hung it by a radiator. She could see from the set of his shoulders and the clench of his jaw that this minor inconvenience had stressed Weiss considerably. His face was the colour of beetroot and he clenched his fists spasmodically; a sure sign of inner tension which Else recognised all too well.

"Sit down and relax. You look like you are on the verge of a heart attack," she ordered. "Calm down and I'll get your coffee."

"Sort out the parking space first. Don't bother with coffee"

"There's plenty of time. The whole day in fact. Here, just relax."

Else stood behind him and reached over to massage Weiss' shoulders and the back of his neck. She chatted about his weekend, agreeing that Lil was right not to share his enjoyment of films noirs. Who was this Robert Mitchum anyway?

By the time she had finished Weiss' mood was undergoing a pleasant renaissance and he was ready for coffee. The only shred of irritation he now felt was due to the chill dampness of his trouser legs. He was ready for coffee and to leave the parking question to Else.

"You're coming tonight?" she queried on her way into the outer office.

It was a sign that the incident of the parking space had affected Weiss considerably that he found it necessary to ask "Tonight?"

"Monday's our night. Monday and Wednesday. You always come round...for a couple of hours."

Thus recalled to the normal flow of his life's routine Weiss agreed that he would be round at Else's apartment as was usual on a Monday evening. In fact he wouldn't miss it for anything.

"That's good. I'll make us something nice, "Else concluded as she closed the door behind her.

Weiss pushed the morning's incident to the back of his mind and pulled the pile of papers from his in-tray towards him. He had nothing particular to do that day, no meetings scheduled and no assignments on hand. He had promised himself a quiet day just catching up on paperwork and routine.

He tried to work but despite Else's soothing and the coffee she brought him promptly, the incident of the parking space still rankled. He shuffled papers around his desk and three times he looked out of his window to see if the offending vehicle was still there. It was.

He sipped his coffee. Else had even brought some biscuits on a china plate. Weiss valued these little luxuries. Else hadn't just brought any biscuits; these were his particular favourites. He munched on one as he read over a document.

Weiss was a stickler for the protocols of the department. He was especially careful of anything that tended to reflect his own status or generated prestige for himself. He valued that parking space. It was a privilege. It was just like he valued this office, at the corner of the building with double aspect windows. His pictures were on the wall. Each carefully chosen and paid for by the department. He enjoyed sitting behind the big rosewood desk, another symbol of his status.

He picked up one or two of the objects that were lined up on his desk. The department liked to award staff with little crystal or plastic mementoes of significant achievements or of participation in high visibility projects. Weiss had seven or eight set out on one side of the desk. He was proud of them. He often fondled them as if they were his own children.

Weiss could be an especially difficult man to work for, it had to be admitted. Although Weiss if asked would say he rather saw himself more as someone who demanded excellence. Weiss didn't think of himself as vicious or a bully, like some of his colleague in his opinion. No, he simply demanded attention to detail and strict adherence to the procedural manual. Behind his back he was known as "By the Book" Weiss and a collective howl of dismay was known to rise up from the lower floors when staff found themselves assigned to one of his investigations.

Those who sat in authority in the Compliance Department didn't seem to mind his approach though. He had been promoted several times and was often singled out for particular congratulation by the Director.

Else came in and cleared away the empty cup and plate. Weiss asked if she had sorted out the parking issue. He was not best pleased to know that she had not, as yet, made any progress. By way of mild admonition he asked for another coffee.

Then the phone rang. Weiss picked up and heard the familiar voice of the Director.

"Weiss, I need to see you."

"Yes, Director. I'll come down straightaway."

"I'm not in my office. I want you to come to me." The Director gave a street address that Weiss did not recognise. He got out from behind his desk and checked the map of the city that hung on the opposite wall. The street was on the western edge of the city in an industrial district. Weiss had never been in that area.

"Come now. And, Weiss, don't tell anyone where you are going," the Director was continuing.

"This seems to be highly irregular. Departmental directive..."

"The directive does not apply in this case," the Director cut in. He seemed rather testy. "And don't tell anyone that you are meeting me," he continued.

"But..."

"You have my authority, Weiss. That should be enough for you."

"Very well. I'll come to you now."

"Don't rush. Leave the office calmly. No fuss. We don't want to arouse curiosity."

"No, Director. I may be a little time. I had to park in the street. Someone has parked in my space."

"I'm not interested in trivia, Weiss. Just get on your way."

"Yes Director. Trivial I agree. I should be about thirty minutes"

The Director hung up and Weiss listened to the angry wasp-buzzing of the dial-tone for a few seconds, speculating on this strange turn of events. Clandestine meetings were not the stuff of daily business in the Compliance Department.

Weiss recovered himself and replaced his own receiver. He recovered his jacket. It was still wretchedly damp but he shrugged himself into it. Else came in with coffee as he hurried past her.

"Where are you going? Don't you want your coffee?"

"I need to go out."

"Was it that phone call?"

"Can't say."

"But why the hurry? Where are you going?"

"I can't say"

"This is very irregular. What do I say if anyone needs you?"

14

"You'll just have to say you don't know."

"Why can't you tell me?"

"Need to know. It's on a need to know basis."

"And I don't need to know? Can I know when you might be back?"

"I don't know. Really. I have no idea."

"Tonight then?"

"Yes. Yes, of course."

"Call me if...Well call me"

"Yes, of course."

As he took the stairs down to the ground floor two at a time Weiss speculated that he had singularly failed to avert any curiosity on Else's part. As he stepped out in the rain he could imagine her conversation at lunch break with the other secretaries. His behaviour was completely at odds with the usual tenor of affairs in the Compliance Dept.

There had been no let-up in the volume of traffic and it took Weiss nearly an hour to reach the location that he'd been given by the Director. As expected the area was run down, scarred by the remnants of heavy industry and acned by dilapidated housing set in terraces. There was no sign of life on the streets.

Weiss looked around for a place that the Director would have been likely to have chosen for a discreet meeting. He was certain that he had found the right area; the Director had told him to come to a particular corner on a cross-road in the centre of the district.

Looking around, however, Weiss could see only a church. The land on the other corners was covered in weeds and the rubble from the buildings that had formerly stood there. This church was the only option.

In the city churches were an uncommon sight. Some, of course, of the most striking and lavishly decorated examples had been kept to attract and please foreign tourists. Yet others were now museums and some of the more modern had been converted to social uses. All of these, however, were located in the central districts. This church was not modern but a throwback to medieval times, with a steeple and faux battlements. It stood like a derelict awaiting the ship-breakers amid a sea of wasteland.

Weiss climbed the worn down steps and pushed on the thick wooden door. It gave easily and opened without a sound, He went in. The place smelt of religion, that musty smell of candle grease and dust and decaying books. There was a priest at the altar; all dressed up like a black crow. There was an old woman too, polishing the floor. He looked about for the Director but there was no-one else visible. A row of confessional boxes stood along one wall. Weiss checked each one. No one.

The priest seemed to finish whatever task had been occupying him and disappeared into an inner room. He emerged a few minutes later now gorgeously dressed in a brilliantly coloured robe over his black garments. He rang a small bell and the old woman scuttled to a seat at the front of the church just below the ornate pulpit that seemed to soar above the pews.Weiss heard the doors open and shuffling feet approaching. He turned to look at the newcomers expecting to see the Director. Instead a small group of soberly dressed men and women, maybe five in total, had entered the church. Weiss watched them as they each found a preferred spot among the pews and settled themselves. The priest began to chant in a high nasal voice and the congregation, such as it was, stood to respond.

Weiss took a seat at the back of the church. He was wondering where in the desolation outside this collection of religious devotees had sprung from when he felt a hand brush his shoulder. It was the Director who had seemingly, himself, sprung from nowhere. He motioned for Weiss to follow him.

They went into a side chapel decorated with the statue of the saint to which it had been dedicated. Weiss noticed the bare feet of the saint were standing on the pincers and other tools which were doubtless symbols of the method of her martyrdom. A large wooden cross bearing the tormented body of a Christ figure loomed over the space. The Director motioned for Weiss to sit and sat alongside him. Weiss felt a momentary discomfort at the closeness of the bulk of his superior. He could smell an odour of earthiness about the man.

The Director was speaking in a subdued tone as the religious service droned a background motif.

"Weiss, I am relying on your discretion and your good sense. I have an assignment for you which will call for resourceful and discreet handling."

"This is very irregular…" Weiss began but the Director laid a hand on his arm and cut him short.

"Just be quiet and listen to what I have to tell you. If time permits you can ask questions when I've finished. Do you understand?"

Weiss nodded agreement and the Director continued:

"Here is a file. Show it to no-one else. It contains highly confidential information." A file had appeared in the Directors hand, produced from within the folds of his thick winter coat.

Weiss fought down strong feelings of misgiving and forced himself to stay silent. This was not how things were done in the Compliance Department. A committee would be formed. A method of investigation debated and adopted. A team assembled. Weiss began to regret even coming to this meeting. But then how do you decline an instruction from the Director?

"Take it then," the Director thrust the red jacketed file at Weiss who despite his reservations automatically reached out and took it. "Well, conceal it. Put it out of sight."

Weiss wished that he had worn a coat or brought along a briefcase. All of this had wrong-footed him. He pushed the file inside his still damp jacket, nestling it in his armpit. The director was continuing to speak:

"Take it away and read it carefully but make sure no-one else sees it in your hands or overlooks you. In the course of this investigation you will report directly to me. No-one else is to be involved."

"I'm to work alone?" Weiss couldn't help himself.

"That is what I am saying. When you have read the file make contact with the parties mentioned in it. They have no suspicion that we – the Department – have this information. Tell them that your inspection is strictly routine. Part of a new programme. Of course they'll cooperate – they have no choice. But then they'll make sure that you see nothing you shouldn't. Make sure you get to them today. Speed is critical, catch them off guard"

Weiss held his tongue and looked blankly at the Director.

"I can see you are uncomfortable with this. Clandestine arrangements aren't usual but in this case…The fact is everything in that file has come from a source inside the company you are to investigate. That's where the need for discretion arises."

"A whistle-blower? Is he in the file?"

"Yes, a whistle-blower. However, he remains anonymous. We cannot risk exposing him or her."

"But…"

"The person will contact you...as necessary. You'll be guided. Trust me."

Weiss was silent. He had no choice but to trust the Director. He had no choice in following his superiors instructions however suspect the approach might seem.

"Questions?"

"It's against departmental regulations for a confidential file to be kept outside the secure room at the department."

"That's not a question."

"I'm not sure that I should be doing this."

"Weiss – I've already said that you have to trust me on this. Come on now – we've been colleagues for how long? I am giving you authority to contravene the regulation. That should be enough. Any more thoughts?"

Weiss shook his head.

"Good. Then go. You leave first."

Bewildered, Ludovic Weiss stood at the foot of the church steps in a state of complete confusion. He had literally been ordered out of his comfort zone and he didn't know what was actually expected of him. He was not a spy or yet a policeman. He was a lawyer by education. A civil servant by employment and while he was charged with enforcing the statutes of the state this was always as part of an investigating team, with proper sanction and authority. Now he was being told to trust his superior and act on his own initiative albeit in a discreet and covert way. He was not even sure that what he was being told to do was strictly legal in itself.

How does one question the direction of a senior figure? Weiss realised with a shudder that he had no reference point. There was no-one to ask, no-one to tell. He felt a pang of envy for the whistle-blower.

Weiss' stomach felt empty. He suspected it was all due to the inner turmoil brought on by the day's events. On further consideration he realised that he hadn't eaten since breakfast. He had even missed his second cup of morning coffee.

Just down the street he saw what looked like a lighted sign. On closer inspection he was pleased to see it was attached to a small but cosy looking café quite at odds with the surrounding desolation.

When he entered the place was empty except for the owner behind the bar counter and a waitress engaged in laying cutlery on the tables. He noticed a couple of booths towards the back of the room, out of sight of the road outside and not overlooked from any angle. He slid into the rear most booth, hunkering into a corner as if to ensure invisibility. The waitress came by and without directly looking at her, Weiss ordered a glass of beer and a sandwich.

When she went away he eased the file from beneath his jacket. He flinched at the sight of its bright red jacket that seemed to scream to the outside world demanding that everyone look at it. He edged it onto his knees beneath the level of the table. From a brief glance he could make out that the file contained hand written letters, some computer printouts and various photocopied pages of figures.

Weiss became absorbed in leafing through the papers and nearly jumped out of his skin when the waitress returned. He thrust the file further under the table but the girl barely seemed to notice as she slid his glass of beer and a plate across to him.

When she had gone Weiss brought the file back out onto the table. He cast a surreptitious glance around the room and bent to the papers again. Fortunately someone had thought to prepare a summary of the contents and the salient facts and placed it in the front of the file. From this Weiss gathered that the trading firm in question had been guilty of many violations over the years, all of which they had been successful in hiding from the authorities of the state.

The café door opened again just as Weiss came to the end of the summary. There was a quiet murmur of voices, like a soft wind stirring grasses and the congregation from the church spread themselves around the room. Weiss decided it was time to go and slipped the file back under his jacket. He would only be safe to read the thing thoroughly at home. Now, however, he had to set up the meeting with the offenders. Yes, Weiss had decided that that was how he should think of them. He would have to meet with the offenders with only the sketchy knowledge afforded by the summary. Probably not a bad thing he thought. With scant knowledge there wasn't much he could give away during the meeting. All in all both he and the offenders would probably be equally mystified by what was happening.

Weiss got back to his car, thankful at least that the rain had stopped and watery sunshine had replaced it. Holding the file open on his lap he telephoned to the company noted on the front sheet and asked to speak to the managing director. He was amazed to find that his call was put straight through and that the voice that answered was actually the managing director and not a secretary set on knowing the reason for the call and on denying him access to her boss. He was equally shocked by the reaction to his request for a meeting.

"Ah yes, of course. Whenever you like. This afternoon about three o' clock? Would that suit you? We have been expecting your call.'

Weiss stammered his agreement, hung up and slumped back in his seat. He noticed that a thin film of cold sweat had formed on his forehead. He had braced himself for...what exactly? A blank refusal to see him? Prevarication? Demands to explain, in detail, his reasons for the actual impertinence of asking for a meeting? All of these were variously the usual preliminaries to a planned inspection by the

Compliance Department. By contrast this had felt like pushing on the proverbial open door.

Weiss realised that he had little time to get to the premises of the trading company, InterTrade, he was to investigate by the time agreed for the meeting. He dumped the file on the passenger seat and set of in a squeal of tyres.

The premises of InterTrade looked perfectly normal. Trucks were pulled up alongside concrete piers that jutted from a long shed which itself was attached to a three floor office block. A pair of trucks was drawn up with engines idling, waiting to take their place when one of the loading dock piers became free. Weiss pulled into the parking spot designated for visitors that was positioned handily by the front entrance to the office block. What was he supposed to do with this file? It lay like a pile of toxic material on the passenger seat. It was threatening and made Weiss feel distinctly uncomfortable every time he glanced at it. He wanted it out of his sight. But where? He didn't have a coat or blanket to cover it. He didn't have a briefcase in which to hide it. He thought about locking it in the boot of the car, but cars can be stolen. He looked around the carpark. Was anyone watching? The actual possession of this damned sheaf of papers in a flimsy cardboard jacket was making him paranoid.

He couldn't sit there all day and the clock on the dashboard was already ticking down to the time set for the meeting. Weiss grabbed the file and holding it close to his chest burst through the front door.

He was expected. A security badge made out in his name was already on the reception desk. A young woman hovered by the inner door ready to conduct him to the meeting room.

"I'm sorry," Weiss began, "I came out in a bit of a rush. Could you let me have a pad of paper — A4 would be good. In fact two would be very helpful."

The receptionist handed the requested stationery to Weiss and treated him to a sympathetic smile and asked if he needed anything else. Weiss sandwiched the file between the two blocks of paper. It didn't actually disguise the file but at least, Weiss felt, it was not so much in evidence. Thus calmed Weiss followed the young woman along a corridor and into the conference room.

The managing director who sat at the head of the long, rose wood, meeting table, greeted Weiss affably and invited him to take a seat at his right hand. Water, coffee, juice were all offered and as if on cue half a dozen men and one woman entered the room and took their seats around the table. Introductions were made. Each and every one of the people around the table appeared bland to Weiss. So bland in fact as to be faceless and, Weiss conjectured, would be unrecognisable outside of the room which gave them a context.

Although unprepared it was straightforward enough for Weiss to set out his requirements for his forthcoming inspection. It was, though, with some relief that he realised that no-one in the room demurred at any of his requests. The faceless group bent over their own notepads and assiduously recorded his every request. It was as though the whole of their operation was an open book and all Weiss needed was to ask to be shown their innermost corporate secrets. Weiss thought cynically that although this was a comfortable beginning, this would change radically when he got too close to some real evidence of wrongdoing.

It was agreed that Weiss would start his inspection on the Wednesday, giving a day's grace for the InterTrade management to gather the initial materials that Weiss had specified. In just over an hour Weiss found himself back in his car, still clutching the file sandwiched between the paper pads to his chest. He speculated on who in the building in front of him might be the anonymous informant and how or when this person might make contact with him. Could it have been one of the faceless group around the conference table? The woman maybe? He sensed, rather than saw a movement outside the car.

One of the faceless ones, a man, had stepped out of the front door and was standing just looking at Weiss. He made no movement when Weiss caught sight of him. He just stood there. Weiss wound down the window and was about to speak when the grey suited man slipped ghostlike back into the building. Weiss wound up the window and drove off.

It was too late to go back to the office. It was already getting dark and Weiss did not feel up to finding a parking space in the street and walking in the still damp evening air back to the building. Instead he drove around trying to make sense of the day and killing time until he could be sure that Else would be home. He needed to talk about this with someone and Else could be trusted to listen even if his story had to be edited to remove the sensitive parts.

Weiss reached Else's flat and sat in the car for a while before climbing the steps up to the second floor apartment. The front of the place was in darkness, no lights in the hallway and none behind the curtained windows of the lounge. Weiss rang the bell and heard the chimes echo in the empty hallway.

No-one came. Weiss stood looking at the door for several minutes before he rang the bell again. Still no sign of life. He speculated briefly that Else might have been kept late at the office. But then she could always have called him. He checked his phone; no message, no missed calls.

Weiss took a walk along the balcony that lead past the other flats on the second floor. At the end he turned back and caught sight of the block warden watching him across the space that separated Else's block from its twin. He returned to Else's apartment and rang again. He peaked through the letterbox into the darkness. No lights showed from the rooms at the rear of the apartment. He checked his watch. He had been there for fifteen minutes already.

He took out his phone and dialled Else's number. He listened to the ringing in his earpiece and the ringing from within the flat. Nobody picked up. He rang Else's mobile number and listened as the recorded voice of the message service cut in straightaway. For a second he considered leaving a message and then cut the call.

Standing there in the chill night air he was struck by the ridiculous nature of his situation. He had a delightful wife and he knew that he loved Lil. He had a pleasant home, comfortable and welcoming. Yet here he was waiting for, not only his mistress but his secretary to let him in for a couple of hours of illicit… what? Pleasure? Intimacy? He was forced to laugh at himself although he suppressed the impulsion to do so out loud.

He felt someone watching him and turned to see the block warden was now standing at the corner of the balcony, by the steps he had mounted from the parking space. Weiss tried the bell one last time without any hope of an answer. He knew he risked arousing the interest of the warden if he continued to loiter at the doorway. Questions would be asked, names recorded.

An inconvenience which might lead to a need for explanations. Best not to provoke it.

Weiss brushed past the warden as he made for the stairs. He descended quickly hoping that he had not made himself too memorable. He reassured himself that Else, when she returned from whatever was keeping her, would be able to explain his presence should the warden prove curious.

He paused at the door of his car and looked up towards Else's flat. He was surprised and not a little annoyed to see a light go on behind the lounge curtains. He debated the idea of returning now that he knew there was someone definitely in the flat. Was that someone in fact Else? Was there a visitor? Someone of whom he was unaware?

The file was on the front seat. He had neglected it in his desire to see Else and unburden himself. A foolhardy move. He realised that now. Was Else as trustworthy as he had assumed?

Weiss dismissed these unwelcome thoughts and told himself that tonight he needed to focus on the assignment and to try to unravel the unsettling events of the last few hours. It was already late. He needed to get home and read the file thoroughly. Tomorrow, he told himself, he would confront the Director when he made his initial report.

It was very late by the time that Weiss reached his own apartment. Lil was already in bed, fast asleep, curled in a foetal ball beneath the duvet. Weiss sat in the darkened lounge with a single table light to read by. He had poured himself a glass of scotch whiskey and opened the troublesome file on his lap. He leafed through the contents and then read carefully and with attention for a couple of hours. The nature of the offenses was quite clearly spelled out and the evidence so far accumulated made a damning case. Weiss began to wonder what more his own investigation was supposed to unearth.

Eventually Weiss found his attention wandering and his head drooped over the file. If he was to be at all effective the next day he must try to get some sleep in the few hours that remained of the night. The question of what to do with the file again bubbled to the surface. After some thought Weiss decided that it would be safe enough locked in his briefcase which he slid under the bed.

Thus assured Weiss climbed under the covers. He put his arm around Lil. She stirred briefly, uttered a soft sigh and was instantly again wrapped in a deep sleep.

TUESDAY

Ludovic Weiss slept badly. Lying next to Lil he tried to come to terms with the extraordinary turn the day had taken. Eventually he drifted off to a dream troubled sleep wherein he revisited the church, witnessing a group of faceless celebrants gathered around a massive altar as a black robed priest, equally faceless, chanted a meaningless liturgy. When his sleep was deepest he suddenly came awake as if projected by a massive and unseen hand into consciousness.

Blearily, through red rimmed eyes, he stared at the bedside clock, and found that he had overslept the alarm. Lil was already up. Weiss found her in the kitchen preparing breakfast.

"You're going to be late. Where were you last night? You were even later than usual."

"The Director wanted me," Weiss half lied. "He needed to brief me. A new assignment."

"What do you want for breakfast?"

"Just toast. I'll eat it on the way."

"Coffee?"

"No time."

Weiss showered and dressed. He grabbed the briefcase from under the bed and was half way out of the door when:

"Don't say goodbye then. And here's your toast."

He slunk back to the kitchen, picked up the warm package of toast and rewarded Lil with a kiss on her proffered cheek.

"No point in asking when you might be home, I suppose."

"No. Sorry," as Weiss closed the front door.

At the Compliance Department building Weiss experienced another blow to his equanimity. Someone had again usurped his parking spot. Angrily he got out of his car and inspected the offending vehicle. It was then that he noticed that the signs designating his proprietorial rights over the space had been removed.

He felt winded, as if a carefully aimed blow had connected with his stomach. He began to tremble with shock. He climbed back into his car and sat for a full minute composing himself. He toured the compound but at that time of day every space was already occupied. He drove to the spot he had found the day before and was mildly gratified to find that it was still unoccupied.

At the office he was annoyed to find that Else was not at her desk. He yelled for her and stormed into his office. She appeared a few moments later, her arms full of photocopied documents.

"What's the matter?"

"Where have you been? "

"I was down the hall, photocopying. Do you want your coffee?" She held out the sheaf of papers she was holding in a placatory gesture.

"Did you sort out the parking problem yesterday? Did you get the car moved?"

"Yes, of course."

"Did you find out who it was?"

"Yes."

"Who was it?"

"You don't need to know. Just forget about it."

"Well, it's happened again. That's two days running."

Else seemed not to understand the gravity of the situation. Was this some form of insolence Weiss wondered? Weiss repeated himself with emphasis.

"Someone's parked in my spot. Take a look."

"A different car. It can't be the same person"

"I don't care about that. They've no right. I worked for that privilege. I had to go and park in the street again."

"Not raining today though." That tone of indifference again.

"What's that got to do with anything?"

"It's green. Yesterday it was a yellow car."

"I don't care what colour it is. Get it moved. And tell whoever it was not to do it again."

Else was turning to go when,

"And another thing. Someone's removed the signs from the wall."

Else rewarded him with a blank stare of incomprehension.

"The signs that say the parking spot is allocated to me. Someone has taken them down. Get them replaced."

Understanding returned to Else's expression, "Ah, you haven't read the memo." Was that an undertone of malice that Weiss thought he detected?

"What memo?"

"From the Director. It came yesterday afternoon."

"I was out yesterday afternoon. Is it important? You should have contacted me."

"You didn't say where you were."

"Need to know. You could have called me at home."

"It's on your desk. I'll get your coffee."

Else left the room. Weiss sat and drew the sheet of paper in the middle of the desk towards him and read with astonishment. He was informed that in line with a policy decision, his parking privilege had been withdrawn. Henceforth, the memo stated, he was permitted to park on the campus in any free space. As Else had said, the memo was signed by the Director.

Weiss felt himself abused. How could the Director do this to him? The same Director who had demanded his trust and had entrusted him with the burden of an assignment beyond the norms of the department. So this was a measure of what the Director really thought of him?

Else returned with the coffee, placing the cup on Weiss' desk. Weiss looked up at her.

"This is outrageous. He's withdrawn my parking spot. No reason. Just withdrawn it."

"I know. I read it."

Still the same unsympathetic tone. A blankness. Maybe, Weiss told himself, she didn't understand the gravity of what had been done to him. The awarding of a privilege, any privilege, was to be prized as a sign of approbation, a sign of inclusion. The withdrawal of a privilege was likewise a rejection. Was he being pushed out of the fold? He recalled another recent rejection.

"Where were you last night?"

"At home." The same casual and indifferent tone.

"I came round. As usual. It was Monday."

"Did you?"

"You know very well that I did. It was Monday. I rang the bell. You didn't come to the door."

"Did you?" now verging on insolence.

"And I phoned you. No reply."

"I didn't get a call."

"It was Monday."

"What about Monday?"

"It's our evening. Monday and Wednesday. Why am I explaining this?"

"You didn't knock."

"I rang the bell. Several times. I waited. I waited fifteen minutes. I went away when the block warden started giving me looks."

"Drink your coffee."

"When I drove away I could swear I saw a light in your living room."

"Maybe there was."

"Wednesday then?"

"That won't be possible. My mother is staying."

"You didn't mention this before."

"Should I have?" Else turned on her heel and walked out. Weiss heard the scrape of her chair as she took her position behind the desk.

He needed to talk to the Director anyway, Weiss reasoned with himself, as he reached for the telephone. I can sort out this parking situation and get some clarification on this assignment. It's not good enough being expected to grope around in the dark.

Mart's gangling figure appeared in the doorway. On any other day, at any other rime, Weiss would have been glad to receive a visit from his friend. Mart was the sort of character that brought light into a room. Obviously Weiss' expression told a different story today.

"Ludo, how's it going? You look like a wet weekend. I thought you might be pleased to see me. You were missed yesterday. What became of you?"

"Out. I had to go out, on business."

"We heard that you were just skiving off."

Mart lounged into the office and propped himself on one of the filing cabinets. He ran his fingers through the mop of straw coloured hair that flopped across his forehead. He grinned.

"Who said that?" Weiss was irritated and defensive.

"That was a joke. I'm pulling your leg. No-one said it."

"Are you sure?" It didn't sound like a joke to Weiss. There was definitely a bite to Mart's tone.

"Of course. Might have thought it..." Again a sting.

"I was on business."

"What's got into you today? I'm fooling around. But we did miss you. Thought you might be around for lunch. And we went for drinks at the Annex. The Director actually stood a round. You did miss out."

Now that really hit home. The Director drinking with the crowd when he was conveniently absent. Something was going on behind his back. Then there was the memo. Weiss handed the offending piece of paper across the desk.

"Have you seen this?"

Mart glanced at the memo and handed it back.

"Can't say I have. That's bad luck, damned bad luck. Compound's full so I suppose you'll be parking in the street. No wonder you've lost your sense of humour."

Mart's voice betrayed him. He was too casual in his response. Of course he'd known, probably the entire department had known. He couldn't have cared less.

"You've kept yours?"

"Yes. As a matter of fact, yes." A touch of defiance? Definitely a lack of sympathy.

"I see." Weiss glared at his colleague.

"Anyway, what I came about," Mart resumed. "The Director asked me to drop by. He wants the file back."

"You know about the file?"

Weiss was astonished and not a little annoyed. The director had been at such pains to emphasise the confidential nature of the file and now he was sending an errand boy to collect it. Weiss was beginning to distrust everything that had gone on yesterday.

"Red jacket – that's what he told me," Mart was continuing.

"And he wants you to take it with you?" That's not going to happen, Weiss told himself.

Mart shrugged his shoulders. "He wasn't too explicit. Take it to him yourself if it makes you feel better."

"I'll do that. Is he there now?"

"Gone to a meeting. He's probably there until lunch."

So that was why he had to send Mart. The Director was tied up in a meeting and wasn't free to make a call. Still, he must need it urgently. Weiss relaxed and rewarded Mart with a smile.

"What about lunch? See you and Gerd about midday?"

"Don't think I will. Got a lot on." Was that a shifty look that Weiss detected?

This was quite out of character for Mart. Lunch was the highlight of Mart's day. Mart's first thought on arriving at the office was to check on the day's menu at the staff restaurant. On most day's he could recite the various options from memory. Mart was never too busy for lunch. This was a brush-off.

"And Gerd? Is he snowed under too?"

"Have to ask him yourself." Definite indifference in the tone. Mart was already turning to the door. Anxious to make his exit?

"After work then? Drinks in the Annex?"

"Got to run tonight. Sorry." This over his shoulder as Mart reached the door.

"Darts tonight though. It's Tuesday." This was heresy. Every Tuesday Mart, Gerd and Weiss played darts in the bar across the street. Weiss had forgotten for how many years this had been an immoveable tradition.

"Got something on. OK?" Evasive.

"See you around then."

"Don't forget the file."

"Oh, Mart, just one thing..."

"What's that?"

"Else..."

"Girl outside?" His escape thwarted, Mart turned back into the room.

"Stop clowning about. Serious question. Have you noticed anything about her recently? A sort of coldness..."

"Can't say I have. You worried about you and her?"

"It's nothing. Just a passing impression."

"You want to get all that under control. People will start speculating about your...stability."

"Do you think so?"

"See what I mean? Anyway got to go. Damn bad luck, about the parking. You ought to have a word about it with the Director when you take him the file. Maybe it was a mistake, clerical error. See you around."

"See you."

Maybe there was something in what Mart said, Weiss told himself. It was this whole affair with the file, the clandestine meeting, it had destabilised him. Of course there was nothing going on behind his back. The whole parking place incident was just trivial and probably a clerical error like Mart said. And why shouldn't Mart have other plans for a Tuesday night? Probably a girlfriend he wasn't letting on about, just yet. And Else was probably in a tizzy because her mother had descended on her. Everybody had their problems. It wasn't all focussed on Ludovic Weiss.

Right now Ludovic Weiss's problem was to get the file back to the Director. Nothing simpler. The director probably needed it to get approval for the assignment or some bureaucratic necessity. Weiss snapped open the catches of the briefcase. He rummaged under the papers he had put on top of the file to hide it from casual oversight. The file wasn't there.

In a panic Weiss up ended the case and tipped the contents onto his desk. He felt in the pockets which were too small anyway to hold the file. He fanned the papers across the desktop. Where was the damn thing? He could have sworn that he had put it in there last night. It must have been still in there when he left the apartment. Obviously he had taken it out of the case and left it somewhere but it must still be in the apartment. He had been distracted, troubled. The whole conversation with Mart had demonstrated that sufficiently. Maybe he had even only imagined calling at Else's.

He picked up the phone and dialled his home number. He might just catch Lil before she left for work. Weiss was relieved when she picked up after just three rings.

"It's me. I need you to do something."

"Hello Ludovic. What's the matter? You don't usually call during the day."

"I need you to look around, in the kitchen, the lounge. See if you can see a red file. A file with a red cover."

Lil put down the receiver. Weiss could hear her moving around the apartment. He heard her steps as she came back to the phone to tell him she couldn't find anything.

"No? Look in the bedroom, bottom of the wardrobe. I'll wait."

Again Lil stepped away from the phone and with growing impatience Weiss heard her moving around. Doors opened and closed. Lil came back to the phone. There was nothing in the wardrobe or anywhere in the bedroom. Weiss told her to try his desk. Finally:

"It's locked? Yes, of course it's locked. I'll have to come home. Yes now. About half an hour."

When Weiss hung up he became aware of a subdued conversation going on in the outer office. His friend Gerd was talking in an undertone with Else. Weiss caught the odd phrase – "never fitted in", "an issue of trust", "only tolerated". Weiss called Gerd into his office.

"What were you saying to Else, Gerd?"

"What? Oh nothing. Chit chat, that's all."

"Who doesn't fit in?"

"Who?" Definitely defensive. Weiss was certain he saw Gerd's cheeks redden.

Weiss persisted, "You were saying that someone didn't fit in. To Else."

"Don't recall." Gerd averted his gaze for a moment before he looked Weiss in the eyes. It was just enough

42

to convince Weiss . "You maybe misheard. You know what they say about people who listen to other peoples' conversations."

For Weiss there seemed little point in pursuing this and he changed the subject. "Have you seen Mart?"

"Yes, of course. He sits with me downstairs, doesn't he?"

"Is he alright?"

"Far as I know. Why?"

"He seemed a bit offhand, earlier. Not lunching."

"That all?"

"You lunching? I've got to get home but I'll be back in time for lunch."

"Sure, maybe."

"Yes or maybe?"

"One of those. Swing by my desk when you get back."

"What about tonight? Mart can't make that either."

"No, er, neither can I as a matter of fact."

"But we always play darts at the Annex. It's Tuesday."

"Need to be elsewhere. That's all."

"You and Mart?"

"Thought we'd try somewhere new. Make a change."

"I'm not invited?"

"You can come if you want."

"Doesn't sound as if I'm needed."

"Please yourself. I've got to be going. It's getting busy downstairs."

"Alright. Lunchtime? Maybe?"

That was enough for Weiss. Gerd hadn't even said a farewell, just turned and left. He was being frozen out, that's what was going on. Those few phrases about not fitting in, being tolerated, they were about him. But what had he done to deserve this? Had there been rumours? But about what? What had he done to turn friends and colleagues of many years against him? Could he trust Else? He needed to trust someone. Was all this in his head? He called her in, made her take a seat.

"Is something going on? Something behind my back?"

"Strange question."

"I've got a feeling, that's all. More than a feeling, actually."

"You should be careful. You don't want to give the impression that you're paranoid."

"What's that meant to mean?"

"Imagining plots...conspiracies...vendettas."

"I only asked if something was going on."

"Nothing's going on."

"Gerd and Mart were both distinctly stand-offish. We always go to the canteen together. We always drink in the Annex. We always play darts on Tuesday.

Suddenly that's all off. And they are both acting mysteriously."

"You're imagining. A night in, with your wife – that's what you need."

"Then there's you. I've just remembered. Your mother died ten years ago. You told me."

"Did I say my mother was staying? It's my sister. Slip of the tongue."

"You've never mentioned a sister."

"What is this? An interrogation? I don't have to tell you everything?"

Weiss was on the back foot now. He could only agree. Apologise. Else was making sense.

"Need to know. Right?" Else concluded.

"Coincidences?" She was making sense, Weiss was calmed.

"It's possible. Why don't you talk to them, Mart and Gerd? It'll be nothing."

Of course Else was right. He was being irrational and this was something for later. Right now it was a question of locating that damned file.

"Thanks Else. I expect you're right. But look, I've left something at home. I've got to go and fetch it."

"You're going home then?"

"Yes. I won't be long."

"What shall I say if anyone wants you?"

"Just that I've gone home and will be back soon."

Nothing else?"

"Nothing."

****

Even on the threshold of the apartment Weiss knew that someone had been there not long before. Maybe there was a slight displacement of the pot plants on the window ledge. Stepping into the hallway he could smell a subtle disturbance of the dead air in the apartment. He told himself it was just paranoia. The job really must be getting to him.

He flipped open the cover of the intruder alarm. It had not been set. Lil would never leave the apartment without setting it. It was one of her pet obsessions.

Weiss called Lil's name. No response. She had definitely left for her own work, probably straight after his call.

Weiss was familiar with the ploy. He had used it often enough himself when he was a field inspector. Judiciously used it would have a suspect running to confess.

He moved into the living room. The disturbance was even more palpable there.

Weiss went straight to his desk. He noted the subtle displacement of the objects he kept on the desktop. Not something Lil would have done while she was searching for the file. He unlocked the drawers and pulled them open. Nothing apparent except a cigar box in which he kept certain private letters had been moved from under the blank legal pads where he kept it and placed on top of the stationary pile. Of the red jacketed file there was no sign.

Weiss locked everything up and checked that the drawers were all secure. He checked in the bedroom, pulling back the bed covers and tossing the pillows on the floor. He checked wardrobes, pulling out the shoes from the floor of wardrobe, laying it bare. Nothing.

In the kitchen he was starting to remove tins from the store cupboard when he stopped himself. This was ridiculous. There was absolutely no way in which he would have placed a confidential file anywhere except under lock and key. He didn't have a safe so the desk was the likeliest place and it wasn't there. Or in the locked briefcase he had placed under the bed.

So had he imagined the whole thing? But the file must exist or else why was the Director demanding its return. Was he going out of his mind? Was he hallucinating? Or had some subtle intruder taken the file during the night as he slept. Of all the options this latter seemed to Weiss the most terrifying.

The fact remained that he was convinced that the file was no longer in the flat. Either it had been taken, an option that Weiss could not accept because the implications and the consequences were too awful to contemplate or he had left it somewhere and imagined or hallucinated or dreamed that he had had it with him in the apartment.

This option, although hardly believable to Weiss himself, seemed more acceptable and he felt compelled to pursue it. He had no better option.

Weiss drove as fast as the late morning traffic permitted and eventually arrived back in the area where he had met with the Director. He was relieved to find that the old church was still standing on its corner surrounded by debris and dereliction. He was shocked, however, when on closer inspection he saw that the windows were all boarded up and a heavy chain and padlock secured the door.

He made a circuit of the outside of the church and found no way of entering. There was only a side door and that too was securely locked. There were no signs of life and the whole place seemed to have remained untouched for many years.

Looking down the street Weiss saw the café sign which was still lit up. As he got nearer he could see lights on in the interior and he experienced a mild sense of relief when he saw the figures of the waitress and the owner inside.

He pushed open the door and went in. As before the waitress was engaged in setting tables for the lunch time trade and the owner was behind the counter. There were no customers.

"Back again so soon? We must have done something right."

"You remember me? From yesterday?"

"Of course. Not that long ago. And we don't get that many customers like you?"

"Like me?"

"Smart suit. Collar and tie. You from the State? Land surveyor? Tax?"

Weiss tried to brush away the enquiry with a smile and a curt laugh:

"No, nothing so grand. No."

"Beer and a sandwich then? Same as before?"

"No, not today. But a question..."

"Like that is it? I'm disappointed," and the owner turned away.

"On second thoughts, I could do with a beer. Been a difficult day."

The beer was drawn from a tap on the bar and the glass placed in front of Weiss.

"Now, you had a question?" the friendly tone had found its way back into the owner's voice.

"About the church, up the road there..." and Weiss gestured in the general direction of the building.

"What about it?" Cooler now. Guarded.

"It's all shut up now...today I mean...but is it ever used...for services? Is there a priest?"

Weiss was sure that the shadow of a glance passed between the café owner and the waitress who had

49

come up to the counter and was standing beside him. Was it guilt? Evasion? Or maybe it was complicity.

"It's been shut up for years," the waitress volunteered. "Never used. No priest."

"But I was there yesterday. I was inside. There was a priest. There was a congregation. They held a service."

"Sorry friend, you're mistaken," there was a hard edge to the café owner's voice.

"When I was in here, the congregation all came in here. They sat at those tables."

"I don't think so. Would you like another beer?"

Weiss could not mistake the note of dismissal in the café owner's voice. He placed some coins on the counter, mumbled thanks and made for the door. He was just about to leave when he recalled the real reason for coming there. Weakly he posed his question:

"Did I leave a file here, when I was here yesterday? It had a red jacket."

"The one you were reading under the table?" This from the waitress.

Weiss realised that he hadn't been as subtle as he'd thought. The whole world probably knew about the damned file. The owner was speaking:

"No, you didn't. We would have given it to you when you came in, if you had. What sort of people do you think we are? Anything else? Fine, then close the door behind you. Need to keep the heat in."

At least, Weiss told himself there was evidence that he had been here the day before. Probably the people at the café had something to hide. They had obviously spotted that he was some sort of official and in these parts that would make any question he asked suspect. They were bound not to give him any information. They were, on the contrary, bound to supply any official of the State with a misleading fabric of lies. But he had been there, that much was true. So why hadn't everything else he recalled actually happened?

The stark realisation that he was still no further forward in locating the file cut through his relief. He climbed into his car and stared out of the window, pondering his next move. The file couldn't be in the church, he'd only just been given it there. Then the café people had confirmed that he had had it there. Maybe it was somewhere in the car. Weiss checked the glove box, peered under the seats, lifted the mats. Nothing. He opened the boot. Likewise nothing. In the engine compartment? No sign.

Weiss concluded that the file must have gone missing sometime after he had visited Intertrade. So that must be the next place to look. He comforted himself with the knowledge that the file's existence and the fact of it being in his possession had been corroborated. It was but a short step to confirm to his own satisfaction that he had actually received it from the hands of the Director. He had not imagined that interview in the side chapel. Whatever else had been going on inside the church was an irrelevance.

By the time that Weiss parked in the visitors' reserved slot outside the Intertrade building the evening twilight had begun to set in. A different girl was seated at the reception desk and Weiss had to explain to her who he was and the bare facts of his conference with the management team the day before. To his enquiry about the red covered file he received a shake of the head. Likewise he was informed that all of the people who had sat around the conference table yesterday were unavailable, were not even in the building. Perhaps he should come back tomorrow when he said he would be expected. Maybe the file would have turned up by then.

Weiss knew that he had come to the end of the trail. Now he was sure that the file had been taken from the apartment under his nose or more properly from under his supine, slumbering form. The little hints that had been left by whoever had taken it were a sure sign. He had only been fooling himself by allowing denial to set him on this fruitless pursuit.

A movement outside the car, from just behind him, made Weiss turn in his seat. A man was standing just beside the rear door of the car, looking at him. In the gloom Weiss couldn't make out the man's features but he was fairly sure that it was the same man who had been observing him yesterday.

By the time that Weiss had stepped out of the car the man had turned on his heels and was walking briskly towards the loading docks. Weiss called after him. This only made the man increase his pace. Soon he broke into a run with Weiss matching him stride for stride but unable to make up ground. The man slipped through a metal door at one side of the loading dock, disappearing into the interior of the warehouse. Weiss tried the door and it opened easily, much to his surprise.

He just caught a glimpse of the grey figure as he disappeared along a corridor and through an internal door. Weiss was about to give chase when two men in blue overalls appeared from among the long rows of steel shelving. They confronted Weiss with a challenge:

"What are you doing in here? Restricted area this is."

Weiss produced his Compliance Department warrant card and the men became instantly polite and accommodating. Weiss cut across their apologies.

"Where does that corridor lead?"

"To the offices."

"Did you just see a man come through here and go down there?"

Heads were shaken in denial.

"I need to know who he is. You didn't see him? You're sure?"

The men were sure. Weiss pushed past them and ran down the corridor. He burst through the door into an open plan office space where several clerks sat at computer screens. They all looked up at the noise and violence of the intrusion as Weiss ran through the space and passed through another door. Beyond he found himself in a corridor which branched left and right. Which way had his man gone?

Weiss was not left to ponder his options. Two bulky men appeared in the corridor and grabbed Weiss by the arms. They ignored his protests and brushed aside the departmental warrant card that he still held in his hand. They frog-marched him through the corridors and through the reception area and ejected him into the cold night air. They left him without a word and took up position on either side of the entrance doors, arms folded across their chests in an aggressive posture. They stared at Weiss until he slunk away.

Out of breath and sweating with the unaccustomed exertions Weiss returned to his car. A scrap of paper had been placed under the wiper blade. Whoever had placed it there wanted Weiss to meet them at certain bar and gave directions. Weiss was to take a seat at the far end of the counter, facing the street door, by the entrance to the washrooms. Weiss was to be at the bar in thirty minutes.

Weiss got to the bar in good time and took his seat at the counter as directed. He nursed a glass of beer, looking up in anticipation as each new customer came through the street door. These were the first moments in the day when he had not been careering around the city in pursuit of the file. His mind drifted over what had happened to him, trying to make sense of what had become a tangle of sensations and impression.

First of all there had been that man in the parking lot. What was he doing? Was he the whistle-blower? Was he trying to make contact? Or had he been a blind for the real insider so the note could be slipped under the wiper blade. The questions nagged at him until they formed a knotted tangle in his head.

He would have dearly liked to have cornered the grey man and found out just what game he was playing. Then there was the turnabout of attitudes at Intertrade itself. Yesterday he was as welcome as could be; the red carpet had been rolled out for him. Today he had been denied entry, totally forgotten and ejected with some violence.

Weiss was sure now that he was being watched. He scanned the bar. How could he pick out his shadow? That was the nature of the process. The bar was getting pretty crowded with the after work clientele. It could be anyone. The business man at the bar, the couple in the booth. Whatever he could see, Weiss felt eyes upon him.

His thoughts drifted to Mart and Gerd. They were definitely behaving oddly. Their attitude towards him had hardened. It had an edge. He almost felt threatened by their apparent indifference.

He kicked himself mentally. All of this was getting to him. This was all of his own imagining. They had been pals for years. They knew each other's families, spent time together. Joked together. New each other's secrets. He'd end up suspecting Lil next. What a laugh!

But then there was Else. What was going on there? If she wanted to stop their Monday/Wednesday thing, it was of no consequence. She only had to say. He would be quite glad, if he was truthful with himself. It had been getting stale just recently. Pity because she was a good PA. He shouldn't have started really but it had been tempting. And it was on offer and that didn't happen every day.

Weiss, deep in these speculations, had been unaware of the customer who had come through the door. An envelope landed in his lap below the lip of the bar top. He looked up. He was sure that the woman beside him had been the one in the meeting room yesterday. He couldn't remember her face but the blonde hair and the figure were right.

"Look away. Ignore me," pitched just above a whisper.

The woman was gone, into the washroom. Weiss palmed the envelope into his jacket pocket. He emptied his glass. Should he wait for the woman to return? He wished he'd got a better look at her. He waited a couple of minutes. The barman was looking at him. Soon he'd come over and ask if Weiss wanted anything else. He wished he knew what he was supposed to do.

He slid from his stool. Maybe the woman was waiting for him at the back of the bar. He went through the door that led to the washrooms. There was no sign of anyone. He checked the men's room. Nothing. Of course there would be nothing. Weiss decided against checking the women's area. He opened the door to the alley behind the bar. There was no-one there. He checked behind the dustbins. The woman had disappeared into the night.

Back in the bar he hesitated again. Should he just leave now or wait some more? Maybe she'd come back. He was conscious that this indecision was making him look suspicious. He decided he had nothing to lose and maybe something to gain by staying. Weiss slid back on his bar stool and signalled to the barman. Another drink wouldn't go amiss; it had been distinctly cold out there in the darkened alley. The barman was asking what he could get for Weiss. He was tired of beer, wanted something to kill the chill. He ordered a brandy, made it a large one.

The fiery liquid was just what he needed. It slipped down easily and he was on his second glass before he realised it. A figure out in the street paused in front of the window. A face was pressed to the glass, looking in. The figure came to the door and came into the bar. Weiss recognised the grey man from the car park. The man looked about him as if trying to find someone, then turned and left. Weiss knew he should follow.

He drained his glass and slid from the stool. He left money on the bar and went out into the street. He shivered as the chill hit him and drew his coat around himself. It had become quite dark in the street outside. By contrast with the light and liveliness of the bar, the street was deserted. There had been a rain shower while Weiss had been inside. The pavement glistened and puddles had formed where some of the paving stones had cracked and deformed.

Weiss looked up and down the street. There was no sign of the man. He must have moved quickly or was he lurking somewhere in the shadows? Was he friend or foe? Weiss chose a direction and started to walk away from the bar, slowly, trying to make out any figure that might be standing in the darkness. He was sure there was someone behind him. He turned, unsure, but there was no-one there. He continued on his way. What was that noise behind him? Footsteps, he was sure he heard footfalls. Again there was no-one behind him.

He quickened his pace. The footsteps behind him became faster likewise. He wanted to look back but was afraid of what he might see. He was almost breaking into a run. The blood was pounding in his ears.

The first that Weiss knew was the kick to the back of his knee that chopped his leg from under him and sent him tumbling to the pavement. He splashed into a puddle as a heavy boot connected with his ribs. Hands rifled in his pockets, found the envelope. He raised himself on one elbow and another kick to the shoulder returned him to the ground.

"That's enough," a voice growled and running steps receded into the darkness.

Weiss got to his knees in time to see two indistinct figures round a corner and disappear.

A man and a woman, walking hand in hand, were approaching from the opposite direction. Weiss dragged himself to his feet and staggered towards them. He saw them cross the street and hurry by on the other side. He was dizzy; he staggered backwards and caught himself against a shopfront.

****

Weiss let himself into the apartment which was in complete darkness. He dragged himself into the living room and poured himself a healthy glass of scotch. He tossed his sodden jacket onto the sofa and slumped into a chair. It was only then that he began to wonder where Lil might be.

He realised that he had no idea what Lil might be doing and where she might be at this late hour. The living room clock stood at a little before eleven o' clock. Normally he would be getting home from his evening with Mart and Gerd, playing darts and fooling around at

The Annex, round about midnight. Lil had said something about an evening class but such classes didn't go on this late.

Sleep overcame him and it was some time later when Weiss came blearily awake. He had spilt the best part of the glass of scotch over his trousers and let the empty glass fall to the floor. His ribs were starting to throb and the back of his knee was painful. He dragged himself upright and staggered to the bedroom. He tossed his clothes onto the floor and climbed into the bed which was still unmade after his frantic searches of the morning. Weiss didn't so much sleep as become unconscious.

WEDNESDAY

There was a bitter taste in his mouth. His eyes felt gummy, the lids glued together. He reached across the bed and felt cold sheets that had not been slept in. Where was Lil?

As soon as he moved the pain in his ribs started, He levered himself upright and forced his eyes to open. His clothes were still in the crumpled ball on the floor. The room smelt of stale alcohol. He realised that he was naked beneath the sheets. Where was Lil?

His stomach churned. He stumbled to the bathroom and dry retched over the sink. In the mirror he saw the bloodied gash on his cheek. He remembered that his face had hit the pavement just before the kick in the ribs. A bruise as big as a tea plate had formed over his ribcage. Its companion stood in purple and dull yellow glory on his shoulder. Where was Lil?

He found her in the kitchen eating from a bowl of porridge. She cast a cold eye over him. Later, much later he recalled that cold appraisal. Why was she not more engaged by the sight he presented?

"What did you get up to last night?"

Weiss sat and kept silent. The fact was he didn't know what to tell her. Instead:

"You were late last night. Where were you?"

"Don't you ever listen to what I tell you? The evening class. I went to the evening class I told you about."

"But they finish earlier – you weren't here when I came home."

"We went on afterwards. For a drink. We got talking about the class. I didn't think it mattered. You always get home late on Tuesdays. Usually past midnight."

"I didn't go to the Annex last night."

"Unlike you to forego your rituals. Must have been important, whatever it was. So what happened? You look like you've been in a car crash. You haven't have you?" and at last a note of alarm had crept into her voice.

"No. Nothing like that."

"So, you stagger home. The place reeks of whisky by the way. You throw your sodden jacket on the furniture. Spill more booze on the carpet and over yourself, throw the rest of your clothes in a heap and pass out on the bed. It must have been quite a night. So what happened? And don't try to fob me off with all that departmental secret guff."

"When did you get home? Why didn't you sleep in our bed?" Weiss tried to buy time to order his thoughts. Lil had never been this firm before. So this is what it took to set her off.

"I wasn't going to sleep in a pigsty. Anyway that's not relevant. So what happened to you?"

Weiss gathered his bathrobe about himself anxious not to display the bruising on his body. The cut on the cheek could be explained, he hoped, but not the damage to his ribcage.

"It was nothing. I fell over a loose paving slab. I wasn't paying attention. Things on my mind. I fell in a puddle and banged my face. When I got home I poured myself a drink. Probably had a mild concussion. I nodded off and spilt the drink. Then I crawled into bed. That's all it was."

It dawned on Weiss in that instant that they were both lying to each other. To an observer it would certainly appear ironic, maybe even slightly humorous. How many other times? Weiss wondered.

"Well, it's a story. That's the best you've got?"

Lil finished her breakfast in silence.

"I have to go. You'll have to fix your own breakfast. Should I expect you tonight?" Again there was a note of indifference in her voice.

After Lil had left, Weiss poured himself coffee and sat in the kitchen. He didn't have the file. He had been robbed of the envelope passed to him by the Department's covert informer. There didn't seem to be a reason to rush anywhere. He swallowed painkillers and sat, trying to think of something to do next. There seemed no obvious solution. He was trapped in a situation he didn't even understand. He was in a box and couldn't even understand its extent or what it was made of. Eventually he concluded that the only course of action was to let things happen and take the consequences.

When he arrived at the Compliance Department complex he parked in the street close by. He barely registered the fact that the parking place that had been his was now occupied by the same car as the day before. Strange, he thought, how things that once seemed so important soon lost their significance.

Else jumped on him as soon as he entered the outer office. She followed him into his room and barely let him sit before:

"Where did you get to?"

Then she had time to see his damaged face which Weiss had tried to cover with a large plaster.

"And what's happened to your face? You look dreadful. You've had an accident?"

Weiss had been thinking about how to tackle this moment. He desperately needed someone to confide in. Could he trust Else? Was there any other choice? Mart and Gerd he discounted. They hadn't seemed the same people since this situation had presented itself. Was he sure that he could actually trust the Director? He had never considered involving Lil. He was sure he could trust her, but she needed to be defended. But he needed someone who could add perspective to his view. He had no choice. He had to trust Else. He couldn't be alone.

"I've got a serious problem. That's where I've been, trying to solve it."

"I expected you back yesterday but you just disappeared. Off home to get something – you never mentioned what – then you disappeared, went completely off the radar."

Then the whole business was tumbling out of him. Weiss told Else about the file, the clandestine meeting with the Director

"And you took it home? You took a classified file out of the office. Have you gone mad?"

"It was already out of the office when it was handed to me. And I had permission. The Director gave me permission."

"He was among those looking for you."

"I expect he was. He gave me the file on Monday then he wanted it back yesterday. It must be urgent. He's probably wondering what's going on."

"And it's disappeared. Are you sure you haven't just imagined all this?"

"No, it all happened like I told you. I was attacked for crying out loud. Look at my face. I've got other bruises to prove it. I'll show you."

Weiss was on the point of tearing open his shirt. Else took his arm and made him sit.

"Alright, I believe you. It all happened just like you said. So, files don't just disappear…"

"It's been taken. The men who attacked me, they took the envelope the woman gave me in the bar. She must have been our informant. The envelope probably held more incriminating information. I hadn't even had time to look inside. Whoever took that probably also took the file from the apartment."

"I'm sorry, Ludo, but it still seems far-fetched. And you have been acting..." Else hesitated.

"What," Weiss snapped, "I've been acting...what were you going to say?"

"I was going to say you've been acting oddly...for some time now. Obsessive. That business with the parking spot. Paranoia..."

"And the bruises?"

"Maybe you fell. Had an accident. Had you been drinking? Mart mentioned that he was concerned...about you...about the amount..."

"So now I'm a drunk who's hallucinating? Is that the story? Very kind of Mart. If you don't believe me, then go away. I thought you might want to help."

"I'm trying to help you. I think you may have been overworking. Mart was concerned for you that's all."

"If you want to help, believe what I'm telling you."

Just then Weiss heard movement in the outer office and Mart and Gerd came through the doorway. Instantly Weiss wondered how much of his talk with Else they had overheard. Had they been outside, quietly listening to the whole story?

It appeared not as they said hello's and joked with Else. Gerd pulled up a chair and Mart affected to notice Weiss' injured face with surprise.

"Wow. What's happened here? I hope you made sure that the other fellow came off worse." Mart's tone was jocose; the indifference of earlier in the week seemed to have melted away. They were all pals together.

"An accident, that's all," Weiss mumbled. "I tripped on a paving stone."

"And kissed the ground," Mart chuckled. "I told you to take more water with it!" Gerd joined in the laughter.

The remark stung Weiss. So, he had a drinking problem and Mart saw fit to refer to it in that slighting way. What other scandals had his erstwhile friends been retailing about him he wondered?

With uncanny accuracy Mart clapped Weiss on his bruised shoulder. Weiss winced. Outwardly a comradely gesture but Weiss suspected the intent.

"Hurt your shoulder too? No damage to the ribs I hope." Again the friendly pat on the chest had more force than needful.

Else excused herself and went back to her desk. Gerd continued to lounge opposite Weiss. Mart loomed over him, standing at his shoulder.

"So, what became of you yesterday? Apart from falling on your face?"

"We almost missed lunch waiting for you to turn up. " Gerd added, again the tone was friendly. Everybody just good friends.

"And you missed darts. Where were you?"

Weiss was mystified. Surely it was Mart and Gerd who had had better things to do. Better things that did not involve Weiss. Had that conversation taken place? What was going on?

Weiss couldn't keep a note of irritation from creeping into his voice, "I didn't think you were playing last night. You both said you had something else on."

Mart's face counterfeited puzzlement, "You're imagining things. Did you say anything like that, Gerd?"

"Why would I? Tuesday night, that's our night for darts and a few drinks. Wouldn't want to miss it."

"You were missed," Mart concluded.

Maybe he had been mistaken. Maybe Else was right. Then there was the whole thing with Lil. She insisted she had told him about the evening class. Was he having blackouts? Was he not understanding what was being said to him? Misreading tones of voice? He heard himself apologising for letting his friends down, suggesting that next week they would get back to their Tuesday evening ritual.

"Up to you," that tone of casual indifference had returned to Gerd's voice.

Then Mart suggested meeting up for lunch and Gerd went so far as to propose a couple of quiet beers after work.

When they left Weiss sat for some time trying to reason out everything that had been happening to him. Or at least what he thought had happened. Was it all in the mind? His mind? Nobody seemed to be behaving as they had in the past. His friends seemed unfriendly. Mart's outwardly jovial horseplay had definitely had an undertone of malice. And how had Mart known just where to prod and poke? It was almost as if he had been Weiss's unknown assailant.

Then there was Else. She seemed all too eager to foster the notion that it was all in Weiss's mind. He was sure she had been in when he called round. Then there was the tale about her long dead mother coming to stay. And was there really a sister? Weiss doubted it.

He was forced to conclude that Else was not the trustworthy confidante he needed. He had been wrong to tell her about...whatever was or seemed to happening. Certainly he should have kept quiet about the Director and the whole damned business with the file.

So, he was on his own. Or was he? The woman in the bar last night, the woman who had passed him the envelope. There was a potential ally. Yes, he had to find the woman, make contact and work with her. And then there was the Director. He held the truth of all this. Get to the Director, explain about the lost...no, the stolen file and the stolen envelope. The Director was the key; he'd know what had to be done.

Suddenly Weiss felt calmer. He'd made a decision and he had a plan. A simple plan. He smiled to himself at its simplicity. The Director was right there in the building. He could be in front of him, talking privately, getting his guidance in a matter of minutes.

Weiss picked up the phone and dialled the internal number. He listened to the ringing tone for several seconds, heard a click and someone picked up. It was Mart who answered. Of course, Mart sat right outside the Director's office. If the Director was not in or busy Mart would field his calls. Even so Weiss considered briefly whether to proceed. Mart was asking who was there. Hang up or speak?

"Mart, it's Ludo. I need to see the Director. Is he there?"

There was a distinct pause then Mart was talking in guarded tones, seeming to choose his words carefully.

"Ludo, sorry...he's not here at the moment."

"Where is he? When will he be back?"

"Not too sure about that."

"I need to see him urgently. Is he in the building? Can you get hold of him?"

"No, he's not here."

"Can you get hold of him?" Weiss insisted.

A pause then, "No."

Weiss sensed the ice wall in Mart's voice. Talking further was pointless. He hung up. The only way forward was to go and find the Director himself. But then where was he?

Weiss had just concluded that the woman from the bar might be a place, probably the only place, to start, when Else came in with his post. He knew at once that he had to get out without Else realising where he was off to. He had to get some sort of head start before anyone understood where he was going and what he was about. He was amazed at his own cunning.

"Thanks Else." Weiss put on a relaxed smile for her benefit. "How about some coffee? Oh, and do you fancy a Danish?"

"You seem brighter? Has the file turned up?"

"No...but I think I've been imagining things."

"Told you so."

"All back to normal. Probably just too much going on."

"You should learn to take it easy. Relax."

"That's what I'm going to do. Now don't go to the canteen. Go round to the bakery on the corner, I like their pastries better and their coffee's better as well."

When Else left the office, Weiss grabbed his coat and ran down the stairs to the back entrance and took off in the opposite direction to the way Else would be taking. He circled around and retrieved his car. In less than five minutes he was on his way to the Intertrade building.

He reasoned that since he was expected to start on the inquiry today he could easily gain access to the building and once inside he could track down the mystery woman without too much difficulty. He would use the injury on his face as an excuse for starting so late.

At the reception desk Weiss was disabused of his theory. He was not expected and the receptionist denied having seen him before. Production of his official identification papers made no impression. His request to meet with the managing director or any of the senior staff met with a blank refusal. Finally Weiss resorted to asking directly for his mystery woman. This in itself proved difficult as he remembered only the most vague outline details of the woman he was seeking. The receptionist shook her head briefly and denied all knowledge of such a person.

"But you must have someone here like the person I have described. She attended the meeting I had with your management team. She must be a senior manager."

"I'm sorry sir, but you must be mistaken. I have no knowledge of the meeting you are talking about."

Weiss was becoming agitated as his so simple plan began to unravel. He raised his voice and demanded to speak with someone in authority. He did not see the receptionist reach beneath her desk and trigger the silent alarm button.

Suddenly there were two men at his side. They took his arms, pinioning them firmly at his side.

"Is there a problem here, Sophie?" Weiss heard the quiet enquiry.

"I think you should be leaving now sir." from Weiss' other side and Weiss felt himself being propelled towards the door.

It was a mistake. Weiss knew it as soon as he began to struggle and protest. The grip on his arms tightened and a swift punch found his kidney. His feet scraped over the tiled floor as he was dragged through the door and deposited on the steps. Looking up he saw that one of his assailants was the grey man who had observed him the evening before.

"Now sir – get in your car and leave. Do not return, if you wish to avoid further unpleasantness."

Weiss did as he was told and left as fast as his wheels would take him. Now he felt like a chess player who at a crucial point in the game finds himself controlled by his opponent. His every move was predicted, at every turn he was presented with a single choice and every choice lead to an inevitable ending. His opponents, whose identity he could only guess at, were forcing him down a path. It seemed he had just one choice if he was to continue. He had to find the Director.

Of course, Weiss argued with himself, he still had a choice. He could choose to do nothing, to give up. He could turn the car around now, go back to the office or the apartment then sit and wait for whatever outcome would be forced on him. Whatever he did, it seemed to Weiss, the result would be the same. But Weiss wanted to know! And he wanted to know soon. He was tired of the game and he wanted to end it, whatever the outcome. That, he decided, required action on his part. So, he'd take the choice that was offered and drive it to whatever conclusion awaited him.

He knew the Director's house well. He had been there often both socially and on business when he was peremptorily summoned to attend a conference with his boss. It was a large villa fitting the Director's status, in a community of similar imposing residences which stretched along a road that wound through a forest of beech trees.

As he turned into the road off of the main highway Weiss noticed the police car parked discretely among the trees. Two bored looking officers in full uniform sat in the front seats watching the road. As Weiss drove past he noted the two uniformed officers standing by the front gate of the Director's residence. He drove on past the villa, careful to keep his eyes looking forward, keeping to a steady speed. In the rear-view mirror he saw a dark blue car emerge from a driveway and settle on his tail.

Weiss continued to drive steadily but he knew that this forest road would only end at a barrier that divided the metalled road from a forest footpath. He could either turn back and excite suspicion or wait until his progress was halted and he was forced to confront the occupants of the car that was obviously tailing him. He drove on and in just over a mile stopped just in front of the barrier.

In his rear view mirror Weiss saw the dark blue car stop directly behind him, blocking him in. Two men in plain clothes stepped out of the vehicle. One hung back, seeming to cover his companions back, while the other approached Weiss' car. Weiss rummaged in the glove box and found a tattered map. There was a tap on the window and a request for him to step out of the car.

The man was obviously a policeman, even to Weiss unpractised eye. His build and the steel blue eyes that seemed to bore into Weiss's soul without making any sort of human connection were enough.

"This is a private road, sir. Were you aware of that?"

"No…no I wasn't. I was looking for…" and Weiss held out the map.

Ignoring this gesture the policeman continued as if delivering a carefully rehearsed speech:

"Do you have business here? Is someone expecting you?"

"No…I'm trying to tell you…"

"Can you identify yourself?"

A harsh crackling and an indistinct voice came from the dark blue car. The policeman who had hung back called to his companion:

"We're wanted, back there. Now!"

Weiss was no longer of any interest to either of the men. Over his shoulder the blue-eyed one told Weiss:

"Turn around and go back to the highway. Do not stop. Do not return." He slammed his door and the pair took off back down the road.

Weiss was only too happy to comply. He drove steadily back and noted that the dark blue car was drawn up directly outside the Director's house. A group of officers, some uniformed, others in plain clothes were gathered in conference on the pathway. Weiss carried on and re-joined the highway as instructed. He drove to the nearest village and parked at a roadside café.

He had not foreseen the involvement of the police. Were they there for the Director's security? Or to secure the Director? Weiss was unable to bring himself to believe in that second option but thought that he should avoid any further contact with the police until he could be certain of the position. He decided to wait until dark and then circle around to approach the house from the forest. The trees and darkness would enable him to reach the house avoiding anyone who might have been set to watch the rear of the house. Twilight was already setting in and it would be fully dark in under an hour. The café looked like an ideal spot to pass the time. Weiss gathered up the tattered map and stepped inside.

Hot food and a glass of wine gave Weiss a new determination. From his study of the map Weiss found pathways through the beech woods that led, in two miles, to the rear of the Director's villa. He parked the car at a picnic area and grabbed a torch from the glove-box. The night air was cold and damp. Weiss dug out an old parka from the boot of the car and bundled himself in it. As he set out on foot the bruising on his ribs and over his kidneys began to throb reminding him of the punishment he had already taken.

Leaf fall was already well underway in the forest and Weiss blundered along through a mush of wet leaves and overgrown brambles. He was well aware that his progress was not in the least stealthy but after about thirty minutes of stumbling progress natural tiredness forced him to slow his pace. He became more aware of the silence around him, punctuated at times by unmistakeably animal sounds. An owl called somewhere in the forest. He heard the scuffling of animals as they moved out of his way. He thought he made out human forms away to his left so veered right to avoid contact. A form loomed out of the blackness and Weiss threw himself to the ground, rolling behind a clump of bushes.

The shape passed by him within a couple of metres. When it had passed and he was satisfied that he was alone Weiss eased himself to his feet. He brought his breathing under control and began to edge forward until he finally reached the edge of cover about fifty metres from the back of the Director's house.

The rooms at the back of the house were all in darkness. Peering into the pitch blackness Weiss could not make out any human presence. Then a murmur of voices came to him on the still night air. A flame appeared and was extinguished. He was not alone. He'd caught a glimpse of two men standing close together over on his right, about twenty metres away, at the edge of the tree line.

Weiss backed into the woods and stood silently listening. He tried to check his left flank but couldn't make out anything in the darkness. He edged around the perimeter of the open ground hugging the trees, reasoning that if his adversaries were invisible to him he was likewise unseen. He was just congratulating himself on making steady and noiseless progress when his foot met empty air; he pitched forward and rolled into a ditch that ran along the perimeter of the open grounds.

Instantly high powered torch light swept across the ground. Weiss ground his face into the damp earth and waited for inevitable discovery. He heard shuffling footsteps and mumbled conversation just above him. Someone opined that it was a fox making the racket. Another complained of being stuck out in the wilderness for half the night. The footsteps moved away. Weiss waited several minutes before risking a peek above the lip of the ditch. Everything had returned to pitch black stillness.

On hands and knees Weiss made his way along the ditch to the wall of the house. He rolled out and came upright onto a paved surface in front of a French window. He peered into the darkness in the room. A tentative push on the door found it yield easily and swing open. Weiss stepped inside and played the light of his torch along the far wall of the room. There was someone there, sitting in one corner in a wing-backed chair. A table lamp snapped on.

"So Weiss, you're here at last."

The woman had blonde hair and was sitting quite relaxed, her legs crossed. She wore the same formal business attire as on the previous evening in the bar.

"You? Here?" was all that Weiss could manage.

"Why be shocked? Surely you know me by now. Put out your torch like a good fellow. What do you want?"

"I need to see the Director."

"He's not here."

"I have to see him. Where is he?"

"Not here! And you have to go."

Weiss stood rooted to the spot. He felt incapable of any meaningful action He simply repeated:

"The Director? Where is he?"

The woman stood and forcibly turned Weiss to the door.

"Go and go now. You know what's out there. Just run…get away from here, "and Weiss felt a firm hand at his back push him through the door.

Instantly lights blazed from every room at the back of the house. Torch light beams criss-crossed the open ground in front of the woodland. Weiss put down his head and ran straight ahead. He felt himself collide with a body, heard it thud to the ground. He didn't falter but ran blindly on.

He reached the edge of the wood and cowered behind some bushes. His breath came in ragged rasps. His chest felt on fire and bile rose in his throat. He could hear bodies crashing through the undergrowth on either side of him. He had to run. He gathered himself and pelted along a path, saw a figure loom ahead. He jinked right, then left, skirting the figure and plunged onward.

He was sure he heard the crack of gunfire and threw himself down. As he sprawled in the damp leaves he realised that he had heard the crack of a dry branch. No gun play then but there were pursuers close behind.

Weiss crested a bank and saw open ground in a pool of moonlight. He scanned the treeline opposite and made out a structure. Maybe he could go to ground there, wait out the pursuit and then creep away when the scent went cold and his pursuers gave up. He was certain he couldn't keep running. Already his legs were giving under him and his chest was heaving for breath again.

He waited until his breathing approached normal and set off at a jog. He checked over his shoulder. There was no-one in sight. His objective came closer. It was a wooden hut, the door hanging off its hinges. He reached it and cowered inside. He found a pile of sacks. They smelt of manure but he burrowed underneath and listened.

Shouts approached and then the sound of running feet. Weiss held his breath. They were going past; he was going to get away. He relaxed and burrowed deeper into his hiding place. How long should he wait? Until daylight? No. He should move while it was still dark. Where was the car? He had to reach that. Then what?

The sound of voices recalled Weiss to his present situation. There were two of them and they were just outside. A torch beam swept inside and over the pile of sacks. Darkness again but still the mumble of conversation. He heard a sharp laugh. He heard whoever was outside move away. He heard the shuffle of their footsteps and their voices tailing away as they put distance between themselves and Weiss' hiding place.

Minutes passed after the steps moved away. Weiss debated his next move again. Was he safe here? Would his pursuers come back?

In the silence Weiss heard the snick of steel on flint. Someone was out there. He tried to keep himself under control but his limbs insisted on trembling. Weiss smelt something acrid above the scent of stale manure. He was drawing smoke into his lungs. He began to choke. It was getting hot, the heat intensifying quickly. He heard the crackle of dry wood burning. The place was on fire. There was no time for thought. Weiss was on his feet and through the door. He bent double choking and coughing, tears streamed down his face from irritated eyes. He stood trying to draw clean air into his tortured lungs.

In the glow of the flames he made out a familiar face. Then a fist smashed into the side of his face. Dazed he went down on one knee. A sack was pulled over his head and all was darkness again. Handcuffs slipped over his wrists and clicked shut. He was jerked upright and lifted bodily then dumped onto a metal surface. Metal doors ground shut and a diesel engine growled into life.

THURSDAY

Despite himself Weiss slept as the van bounced over forest tracks and then over the metalled surface of the highway. He was woken when he was again lifted bodily from the vehicle and set upright. Strong arms looped through his and he was marched and dragged across pavement and smooth floor surfaces. He knew he was in a building. Felt himself held upright as an elevator swished smoothly up several floors. Again he was dragged along a carpeted hallway and finally pushed into a chair.

He winced when the sack was pulled off him and the bright light hit his eyes. It took several seconds for his vision to settle. He was back in the Compliance Department building, back in his own office. And there was Mart and Gerd grinning at him.

"That was a good chase you gave us. You really ought to get into better condition Ludo. We even gave you a bit of a start." Mart remarked and Gerd sniggered.

Weiss raised his still manacled hands. Mart denied his silent request with a shake of the head.

The artificial light in the office was intense, harsh and cold in its clarity. The blinds had been drawn down tightly and there was no hint from outside of either darkness or daylight. Weiss's head ached and he felt a throbbing in his newly damaged cheek bone.

"Mart gave you quite a shiner there, "Gerd taunted. "He nearly broke his hand."

"Didn't think your skull was so thick." Mart chuckled.

Weiss struggled to make sense of this new situation. Why had his colleagues hunted him down, pursued him like an animal. How could they risk his life like that, there was no need to smoke him out. They knew where he was; they could have come in to get him. What had he done to deserve such malice?

Desperately he searched his memory. This was no ordinary spat among colleagues. No petty falling out about office politics. Whatever he had done, and he already was blaming himself, his transgression must have been serious to turn his good friends against him.

Maybe it went beyond the personal. It must be beyond the personal to make any sort of sense. But what crime had he committed. In those terms his life had been blameless. He was sure of that. Reasonably sure of that. Was there something he had not even been aware of? Some ill thought out dereliction of duties?

The file! It had to be about the file. Should he have reported its absence sooner? Should he have reported the Director's outlandish behaviour? But then who to report to?

Mart was speaking, he held up a briefcase; he was asking if it belonged to Weiss. Weiss nodded agreement.

Mart clicked the locks open and upended the case spilling the contents onto the floor. He turned the papers over with his foot. Weiss was moved instinctively to protest.

"Hey, be careful. What are you playing at?" Weiss tried to stand, to prevent this violation. Gerd pushed him back and he sat back on the chair.

"Now stay there and let us get on. We've a job to do. Leave us to it and it'll be done quicker. Then we can leave you alone. We'll even take off the bracelets. Now where are the keys?"

Weiss was unable to speak.

"We want the keys to your desk. Where are they? I'd just as soon smash it open but keys will be quicker." Gerd continued, patently enjoying the opportunity to humiliate Weiss.

"The keys. Now would be good," Mart emphasised.

Weiss remained silent. Gerd and Mart stood watching him in a silence laden with threat. The situation seemed to have robbed him of his voice. He felt violated. Mart pulled him to his feet and searched his pockets, taking the ring of keys from his jacket pocket. Weiss was again pushed roughly into his seat. Mart used the keys and began pulling out the desk drawers and piling them on the floor.

At last Weiss found his voice and protested the enormity of his treatment:

"What are you doing? There are confidential papers in there. Personal things. My personal things."

He was ignored. Gerd and Mart carried on with their task.

"Why are you doing this? Is this some sort of vendetta?"

Mart seemed to find that funny: "Good word that, eh Gerd. Vendetta. Is that what this is? Eh Gerd?"

"Beats me. He knows a lot of good words. Too smart for his own good, if you ask me," and Gerd added a harsh laugh, like the bark of a terrier.

"Why are you doing this? We're friends. You're my friends. Colleagues." Weiss was pleading.

"Confidential. Isn't it Gerd? Confidential."

"Yeah. Need to know. Confidential."

"Why have you turned against me?"

Again he was ignored.

"That's the last of the drawers. It should be light enough now. Well, don't just stand there. Give me a hand, Gerd."

The two men took an end of the desk carcase each and carried it from the room. They returned shortly and removed the rest of the office furniture leaving Weiss sitting in an empty room; empty except for a pile of drawers in the centre of the room. The pair then started to upend the drawers ,turning out the contents on the floor. Again Weiss tried an ineffectual protest and was again ignored.

Mart and Gerd worked steadily sifting the materials piled on the floors. Mart was obviously in charge and they were both enjoying their task. They arranged Weiss' personal effects in one pile, taking their time to look over the photos of Lil and Weiss' other family. They opened envelopes and checked their contents. Other stuff that in Mart's terms was deemed relevant, although he did not specify to what it might be relevant, was piled in a second heap. The remainder that Mart considered only worth shredding was consigned to a third pile.

Weiss continued to plead for some sort of explanation, some reason for this treatment. Eventually Mart remarked knowingly:

"He doesn't get it, does he? Completely at a loss."

"Wouldn't fancy being in his shoes."

They were like playground bullies enjoying the exercise of power over a weaker boy. The fact that their victim could obviously see no reason for being victimised simply added relish to the occasion. The bullies continued to gloat and tease their prey:

"Shredding pile's big enough. Bit of a hoarder wasn't he."

"Anally retentive, that's what that's called. Up his own arse if you ask me," mean laughter followed this sally.

"You're enjoying this aren't you?" Weiss couldn't keep the hurt and indignation from his voice.

"It's not personal." Mart grunted.

"Don't kid him," Gerd pitched in, feeding his companion like a vaudeville comedian.

"Alright, it's not personal, "Mart admitted. " The order wasn't personal. But we've enjoyed carrying out."

"We're friends. I'm your friend. How…"

"Look, we just tolerated you. Okay? Now shut up whining!"

"Pain in the arse really."

"Glad of the chance to stick it to you," Mart concluded and again they bent to their task.

A tall, broad boned woman arrived and scolded Mart and his accomplice from the room. There was not a hint of the feminine about her. Her mannish look was emphasised by the close cut brush of her ginger hair. She looked around the room and remarked:

"They've really made a mess in here. Let's get those cuffs off you."

She released Weiss and handed him a mug of coffee. It was the first humane treatment Weiss had experienced in several hours. He dared to let himself relax.

"You're a bit of mess yourself, aren't you? The Director's going to be along soon. Take off that horrible coat for a start."

At last. Weiss rejoiced. At last the Director was going to put in an appearance. Now all this confusion would be cleared up. Everything was going to be sorted out. Whatever had been going on would all be explained. Then those sods Mart and Gerd would be in for it.

"Who are you?" Weiss ventured.

"Else. Drink your coffee."

Despite the situation he found himself in Weiss almost laughed out loud. The contrast between this Amazon in khaki drab and the stylish and feminine Else was stark. This man-woman was more like a prison warder than a confidential secretary. In the coming days Weiss would find himself returning to that thought more and more.

"You're not Else."

"I am Else," the woman stated flatly.

"What have they done with her?"

"Nobody has done anything. You need to calm down. Shall I get you something? For your nerves."

"Why did they do that?"

"Who?"

"Don't play games. Mart and Gerd. They wrecked my office."

"It's confidential."

"They wrecked my office and took everything away."

"Not quite everything," gesturing to the piled up debris on the floor. "We'd better tidy up."

The woman who was not Else left the room briefly and returned with a roll of black sacks.

"I want Else. The real Else. Get Else," Weiss persisted.

The woman tore a couple of sacks off of the roll and handed one to Weiss:

"Now stop that. Here. You can help. Put everything in these."

Weiss found himself responding to the woman's clear tone of authority. He opened his sack and got down on his knees.

"What should I do with my personal stuff?"

"I don't care. But put it somewhere. Look, stuff it in the briefcase."

When everything had been bagged up Weiss asked what he should do now. He was already yielding to her authority, becoming compliant, glad to be told what to do. When she said simply, "Wait" he resumed his seat The woman who Weiss was beginning to think of as Not-Else picked up one of the sacks and left.

Weiss was left alone for some minutes. He nursed his wrists where the handcuffs had chafed. He stretched his legs and looked down at the wreck of his clothing. Mud clung to him and the reek of manure rose to his nostrils. He went to the window hoping to see out but there was no chink in the blinds. He felt around the window's steel frame but there was no apparent means of opening the blinds which were sandwiched between an inner and an outer pane of glass. He felt sure that there had been some means of opening them there before. Had someone removed it?

He heard someone enter the room and turned away from the window. It was the blonde woman. She stood looking him over, cool and calm. At some time she had changed her clothes and looked fresh and untarnished by any of the night's adventures

Leaden confusion mined a pit of emptiness in Weiss' gut. He had no idea what was happening to him. He wanted to run, to hide and to deny what was happening to him. He backed away from the woman, into the far corner of the room. He turned his face away and closed his eyes.

"Come along Weiss, this is not doing you any good." The voice was coaxing, reasonable.

Weiss turned to face the woman. She continued to regard him with a steady gaze of self-assurance and control.

"What's happened to your desk?"

"Who are you?"

"You know me well enough, Weiss."

"I don't. Of course I don't. I thought you were one thing. Now you seem to be another," Weiss protested.

"I asked you a question Weiss," the woman persisted, ignoring Weiss outburst. "I'd like an answer. Where's your desk? And the rest of your furniture?"

"It's been taken. Just now. I asked who are you."

"Are you feeling quite alright, Weiss? You know who I am," the woman's voice continued calm and reasonable

"I have never seen you before in my life. What are you doing here? Who authorised you…"

"I'm your Director. I am Head of the Compliance department."

Things were getting beyond unreasonable! Weiss sat back heavily on the only remaining chair. His head spun. First Else had been spirited away and a completely nonsensical substitute offered in her place. Now the bear of a man who he knew to be the Director, his Director, had metamorphosed into a woman. He felt sick and on the edge of passing out. At last he managed to blurt out:

"You're not!"

The woman remained cool and remote. She smiled and shook her head as if disappointed but not surprised by Weiss' reaction.

"They said you were behaving strangely. I'm starting to believe that everything that's been said about you is absolutely true."

So they had been talking about him behind his back. He could well imagine who "they" might be. Else had already given him an indication of what might have been said. It occurred to him that even Else might have been one of those who had been part of some smear campaign, wrecking his reputation.

Whatever lies had been spread about him and his sanity and fitness for duty, that didn't explain what he was now presented with as reality. A reality that he was expected to swallow whole!

"I don't understand. First Else then…"

"Me?"

Had a patronising note entered the woman's voice? Was she pitying him? Weiss was on the point of doubting his own sanity and the evidence of his own eyes. He dug deep in an effort to reconnect with reality. He tried to inject an element of assertiveness into his voice. He was not going to be bullied by this woman whoever or whatever she pretended to be.

"What were you doing in the bar? The other night. When you passed that envelope to me."

"So you do remember that?"

"Of course I do. If, as you say, you are the Director of this department why the masquerade, the play-acting?"

"Good try, Weiss. An excellent question." And she rewarded him with a hollow grin. "It was a diversionary tactic. We saw you blundering about and in danger of wrecking months of careful work. It was just a means of pushing you in a different direction and away from the real issues.

"And I get thumped into the bargain. I suppose that was Mart. He seems to get a kick out of knocking me about."

"I can't possibly comment. I just know that it worked."

Her lack of expression and her refusal to engage in any argument or explanation deflated Weiss. He began to cower mentally.

"But the envelope? There was information in the envelope. Relevant information. Otherwise why take it off me?"

The Director reached into her handbag and pulled out an envelope. She offered it to Weiss.

"Here. See for yourself."

Weiss tore it open and took the folded sheets of paper from it. They were blank. He turned them over. He stared at them. Virgin white paper, folded in four.

"This isn't the envelope. You can't fool me."

"It is. Whether you believe it or not is immaterial."

Weiss crumpled the papers and squeezed them into a ball. The Director continued in the same even, reasonable tone.

"You haven't answered my question. Who did this and why did you stand aside and let them?"

Grudgingly Weiss felt himself compelled to answer. Surely it was this woman who insisted that she was the Director who had authorised the whole thing. She had turned his friends against him and made them her accessories.

"You must know. It was Gerd and Mart, from downstairs. I thought they were my friends."

The Director was smiling and shaking her head in disbelief. She shrugged her shoulders:

"Why would they do such a thing? If they are your friends? Are you sure about this?"

"You set them to it. I don't know what I've done. But you set me up."

"Perhaps it was all their idea. It's certainly handed you a lesson in the nature of friendship. Assuming that that is actually what happened…" The note of disbelief in her voice was palpable.

"The desk's gone. The office is wrecked. I stood here while they did it."

"Are you sure? Sure about what you saw?" her voice insinuating.

"And Else – she's gone," Weiss blurted in desperation

"She's right outside," the tone matter-of-fact.

"That's not Else."

"Ah. I see."

Three words that seemed to hold out a lifeline to Weiss. He was desperate and he would accept any explanation. He needed to understand. He craved an explanation that would unshackle him from the torture in his mind.

"You understand now?   You know what's happening?" he asked with a shred of hope in his voice.

Weiss's relief was momentary.

"No. But you need to calm down and stop throwing accusations around."

"What's happening to me?" Weiss was pleading. He felt tears start from his eyes. He blinked them away and cuffed at the wetness.

"I've no idea. What I know is you failed to protect official materials from some act of vandalism by person or persons unknown," the Director stated baldly.

There was a silence between them. Weiss snuffled as the tears ran down his cheeks. The Director stepped towards him and circled round his seated form. She was not a tall woman but she loomed over Weiss as he tried to withdraw into himself. She stood behind him out of Weiss' eye line.

"Or did you do it all yourself? Is this some petty act of rebellion? You do seem to have difficulty fitting in..."

"No!" Weiss squealed his denial with all the force he could command

"Your office. That desk. They're all privileges. You don't seem to value these things." The Director was in his face now, her eyes boring into him. There was no longer a smile. It had been replaced by a look of cold hatred.

"They did it...Mart and Gerd. You ask them," Weiss whimpered.

"And you just stood back and let them get on with it? Is that what happened?"

"How could I stop them?" finally pathetic.

Again the Director circled around him like a predator stalking prey. She sighed eloquently and handed Weiss a small pocket handkerchief.

"It's not that important.   We have other, more urgent things to discuss. Pull yourself together and be a man. Wipe your eyes." There was a subtext of disgust in her voice.

"You have a file. A confidential file A file that you are not entitled to see." The voice hard now, no longer placatory or friendly. The Director was standing firm and upright, cold and business-like.

"I was given it."

"Who gave it to you?

"I was given an assignment and the file."

"By whom?"

"The Director."

"I am the Director."

This was said in a tone that brooked no argument. He could not let himself acknowledge this woman as head of the Compliance department when he knew absolutely that she couldn't be any such thing. He knew the Director. He had known him for years. It was the director himself who had raised him to the position of seniority he enjoyed. He had to find a form of words though, words that could unlock the interrogation.

It was with these thoughts racing in his mind and confronted by the implacable gaze of the woman that he let himself realise that this was his situation. He was under interrogation. He had rights.

"If this is an official interrogation there should be witnesses. There should be records."

"This isn't an interrogation," the reply was flat and quick. "What makes you think you should be interrogated? Are you guilty of some crime? I'm not a policeman. Why would I be interrogating you?"

"These questions. What you've had done to me. It was to soften me up. It can't be anything else."

"My Dear Weiss, you know that the Compliance Department doesn't conduct interrogations. I think you have been watching too many of those American films you seem to enjoy."

"You are interrogating me!"

"Oh, very well. If you insist. So?"

"I have rights."

The Director's laugh was hearty and booming coming from such a small frame.

"Of course you don't. Not here. Get that idea out of your head. Now answer my question. You are getting tiresome."

Weiss weighed his options. He could refuse to answer, go mute. What would be the consequences? Maybe another encounter with Mart's fist? That was not in the Compliance Department's code of practice but it had happened to him on too many occasions now. Maybe a cell? Until he felt like talking?

He stopped himself. Maybe he was deluded. Maybe he was imagining himself in some dark film scenario. If he cooperated maybe he would be helped. Helped to understand.

"Alright, "he conceded eventually. " I was given it by the man who I have known to be the Director of the Compliance Department for some years."

"Very well. In the interests of making progress we'll let that pass. You say you were given the file..."

"And an assignment. I was given an assignment. A confidential assignment"

"Where and when"

Weiss told the whole story over again. Even as he spoke the tale of clandestine meetings in churches that were active at one point and closed up the next day and of burglaries and beatings seemed far-fetched even to himself. Yet he had lived those events. Or at least he thought he had. He began again to doubt his own sanity.

He started to talk about his visits to the Intertrade offices and his meeting with the senior management team. The Director, who had listened in silence, smiling from time to time and sometimes indicating disbelief with a shake of the head, broke in:

"Ah yes. Let's talk about that. There have been complaints. You have been upsetting important people. Why?"

"I was told to investigate..."

"By some imaginary figure you claim to be Director of this department."

"I was given authority," Weiss insisted.

"Where and when?"

"I've already told you!"

"Ah yes. A pretty tale. Quite unbelievable except it was seen to take place."

"You knew?" Weiss could not believe it. He had been watched, followed, informed on.

"Of course. We've known what was going on for some time. We saw the whole charade work itself out. My only regret is that we let you run around loose for too long. We should have reeled you in before you really got going. That was a mistake and I own up to it. Everyone makes mistakes, though. Don't they Weiss? It was a great pity that we had to improvise our little diversions. Damage limitation. That's the trouble with loose cannons and that's what you are Weiss. Incidentally how did this person you talk of as the director, explain this strange way of arranging things?"

"It was for discretion. He said there were too many eyes and ears in the building."

"You would have done better to be discreet yourself." The Director observed.

She walked over to the door and checked the outer office. She stood looking at Weiss for a while in silence, and then snapped:

"Where is the file now?"

"I don't know. I haven't got it. It's disappeared."

"My dear Weiss, you seem to have a very cavalier attitude to the properties of the department. The valuable properties. The confidential properties of the department."

She let Weiss digest her statement with another silence. She went out to the outer office and brought back a chair. She set it down opposite Weiss and sat down. Weiss was beginning to droop. The events of the previous nights were beginning to tell on him again. His shoulder ached and he was sure his face had swollen. The director placed a hand under his chin and lifted his head so they were looking into each other's eyes. She resumed her questioning:

"So where and when did you last have this file in your possession?"

"I took it to my apartment. I locked it in my desk, in my study."

"You took confidential documents out of the building?"

"The file was already outside the building. When I was given it."

"Save me from lawyers!" the Director sighed. "Very well, you were given a confidential file that had been taken out of the building contrary to regulations. In effect by receiving the file you abetted this illegal action. That makes you equally guilty."

"But I had authority...."

"Then you lost sight of the file? Or did you sell it?"

"No. Of course not."

"What was your price?"

"I didn't sell it."

"You're sure?"

"Of course I'm sure."

The director kept after him now, the questions following each other with machine-gun rapidity

"Are you in your right mind?"

"Yes. Of course."

"I'm beginning to doubt that."

"I am."

"I have evidence to the contrary."

"What evidence. People talking behind my back? Office gossip?"

"Clear evidence of paranoia."

"I am not paranoid!"

"Obsessive behaviour."

"I am not mad."

"You seem easily roused to anger."

"No."

"Did you ever offer violence to your wife?"

"How dare you!"

"Let it pass."

"I am sane, I tell you!"

"Yet you expect me to believe that trusted members of my staff have cleared out your office. That they have stolen your desk. For what reason? And you are accusing not only trusted colleagues of long standing but your friends. Then you expect me to believe that some person masquerading as myself authorised you to investigate businessmen who contribute vastly to the economic success of our nation?"

"The evidence in the file showed them to be criminals not patriots."

"So you admit reading the file?"

"Of course I did. I was given…"

"An assignment. Yes, you said that. The fact remains that you read confidential information. Information that was not intended for you."

"How could I carry out my assignment…?"

"Without reading the file?"

"Yes."

"An interesting argument. But flawed."

"Where is this leading?" Weiss was really pleading now.

"Acceptance. That's the way. Take my advice Ludovic. Accept what you are told. It's the best – the easiest – way. Acceptance is the way that limits pain."

"What's happening to me?" the pain in Weiss' voice was palpable now. He needed to know. He was desperate for some sort of assurance that this nightmare situation would be resolved, could be resolved. He was ready to accept any punishment, he'd plead for it.

"Need to know basis, old chap. You just stay calm"

Weiss was not reassured by her calm tone. All this was easy for her. She had the power; he was the victim, the supplicant. He raised his voice, desperate to provoke some sort of concrete action that might release him from his current state of limbo.

"Prison? Is that where all this is leading?"

The director seemed to find this highly amusing. She threw back her head and let out another of her booming laughs.

"What makes you think you have the right to be imprisoned?"

"You're accusing me of...of what? Of stealing state secrets?" Weiss was allowing himself to get angry and to take a belligerent stance despite his subordinated position.

"Am I accusing you?"

Weiss response was firm and unequivocal; of course he was being accused. And falsely accused. He had only followed orders!

"Prison confers a certain status. Even prison. You'll be expecting a trial next."

"I'm a citizen. I have rights. I am entitled to a trial."

The Director was shaking her head. Her lips held a thin smile. She left a silent pause between each of her next statements, letting their full import wash over Weiss:

"You have no status."

"You have no function."

"I'll take your security pass now and your papers"

Reluctantly Weiss handed over his documents, the proofs of his status, the record of his very being. He hesitated as he drew the security pass from his wallet but he had no option but to comply. The Director demanded his keys as well. With a show of petulance Weiss tossed his car keys and the door keys of his apartment across to her.

"Acceptance. That's the way for you now."

Weiss sensed that the interview was at an end but he still wanted answers. He had issues that needed resolution and he was still seething with the anger that the Director's last remarks had provoked. He knew it was probably foolhardy to persist but what had he got to lose.

"The Director. The man I work for. Where is he? Do you have him? Has he been arrested?"

The woman looked at Weiss in silence. It didn't look like an answer would be forthcoming.

"You can't tell me that I've imagined him or that he's an hallucination. I know he's flesh and blood. And you've admitted seeing us together. So where is he? What have you done with him?"

"Weiss, it's not the time. You cannot know."

"And what were you doing at Intertrade? You were there in the boardroom. You were there at that meeting."

"You are being inconvenient Weiss."

"And the Director's house. Why was it surrounded by police? Were they there to protect him? Or to restrain him?"

"I'd stop talking if I were you Weiss. You aren't doing any good. In fact you're doing yourself quite a bit of harm."

"And what were you doing there? Waiting for me? You said I was expected? "

The Director remained silent. Weiss' anger had run its course. Eventually she said, and her voice held a tinge of regret:

"You really ought to have tried to fit in. Can't trust someone who doesn't fit in."

The Director stood and placed her chair in a corner. She walked to the door.

"Where are you going?" Weiss wanted to know. "What's going to happen?"

The Director turned back and offered a conciliatory smile:

"You've got yourself into quite a mess Ludovic. It's going to take some time to straighten it out. But we'll get to the bottom of it, you'll see. It doesn't help that you complicated matters. You could say you brought this all on yourself. So, acceptance... that's thing. No more outbursts like that, if you please. No more inconvenient questions. Just bear with us."

After the Director had left, Weiss paced the room that had once been his office. Was it now his cell? What should he make of this interview with the woman who claimed to be the Director? Or had it been an interrogation? Quite obviously he was being held under restraint no matter how loose the bonds about him appeared to be. He couldn't leave the confines of the building. He couldn't even leave the floor he was on.

Not-Else came in hauling a heavy suitcase. Weiss recognised it as his own.

"What's this?"

"Your things – clothes, washing stuff."

Clearly he was going to be staying for some time. Still Weiss felt himself compelled to ask why his personal possessions were being brought to him. He did not expect the bald answer:

"Your wife's left you."

"Why would she leave me?"

"Maybe the answers in the question."

"But we were happy."

"You were happy? What do you think constitutes happiness? Maybe your definitions didn't coincide."

"Why now?"

"How should I know?"

"You don't think she found out? Could she have found out?"

"Found out what?"

"About us."

"There is no us."

"Mondays and Wednesdays?" Suddenly Weiss caught up with what he was saying. This was not Else. This was not his secretary and occasional lover. He had never met this woman before in his life. He corrected himself.

"No, of course. You're not Else."

"I am Else," a blunt and firm insistence.

"Where is she? Where's she gone? My wife. Where has she gone?"

"She's at home. The apartment."

"But you said she's left me. Where's she gone?"

"She's gone nowhere. She's staying in the apartment. She sent your things here."

"So where do I go?"

"It's arranged."

As if on cue Mart and Gerd arrived, bringing a camp-bed and blankets which they set up along the wall of the office opposite the window. To Weiss it seemed a natural progression. There was some comfort to be drawn from the knowledge that he was not being removed to some other unfamiliar quarters. Now he knew that he would not be permitted to leave.

After they left Weiss began to unpack his things, using one of the chairs to stack his clothes and placing his other essentials under the bed. Not-Else removed the suitcase and Weiss's personal possessions in the briefcase. She told Weiss to undress and take a shower in the cloakroom along the corridor. While he was cleaning himself she removed the muddied and manure stained clothing. Weiss selected clean clothes and dressed himself.

Weiss sat on the bed. Now he was alone in the silence of the empty floor.

TIMELESS

Time ceased to have meaning for Weiss. The blinds shutting out the daylight or the night's darkness remained permanently closed. The harsh white lights in the office remained permanently lit. He was in a space without shadows.

For a long time Weiss was left alone. It seemed that everybody else who had once occupied the offices on the floor had gone. He had the run of the floor but all the other office doors were locked. Where once his security pass allowed him to pass through the grille at the end of the corridor he was now barred from leaving. His place of work had been transformed into a sort of prison.

The psychological blows he had received in quick succession had floored him and drained any reserves of energy from him. The only place of comfort available to him was the bed so he lay there for some hours. He was exhausted anyway so he drifted off to sleep.

On waking he found he was still alone. He lay on the bed listening to the noises of the empty building. The air-conditioning throbbed gently in the background. Squeaks and creaks emerged irregularly. He thought he heard doors bang on floors below as cleaners and security men made their rounds.

He got up and made his way to the washroom. He sluiced water over his face and peeled the plaster from his wounded cheek. The cut was starting to heal over. On the other side of his face a purple bruise was forming where Mart had punched him. He felt his nose. He was momentarily pleased to find that no damage had been done. He relieved himself in the urinal. He listened as the regular fall of cleansing water cascaded against porcelain.

He walked the corridor as far as the security gate. He had not paid much attention to it before. With his security pass he entered and left unhindered. Now he saw that the steel structure was bolted firmly to the wall and completely blocked the access from floor to ceiling. He tried the gate and found it immoveable. This he knew already and wondered grimly why he had even bothered to test it.

He tried the other doors in the corridor and found them all locked. There was nothing on the desk in the outer office to distract him. There were no documents left lying around, no well-thumbed paperback to occupy his mind. He was alone with his thoughts. And the thoughts were unwelcome. There were too many questions and seemingly no sensible answers.

Lil had left him? That was a concept he struggled to process. He searched his mind for clues. There been no obvious domestic rift. He recalled the weekend with crystal clarity. They had been happy together, enjoyed the time in each other's company.

Had what had been happening to him in the last few days been the trigger? He couldn't imagine that that could be the case. Lil understood about work. She understood the dedication that was needed to secure and maintain a position like his. She certainly seemed to enjoy the fruits his labours.

Maybe she had found out about Else. The real Else that would be, not this beefy woman who had been foisted on him as some sort of ad hoc gaoler. If he knew Lil she would not have held back; she would have come at him directly with accusations and retribution. Once again he found himself wondering what he really thought he had been doing in that regard. Else had been a complete act of madness.

Weiss shook himself. He told himself to pull himself together. He had bigger things to worry about than what was probably a temporary marital tangle. If he was right the nightmare situation he now found himself in could well result in his never tasting freedom again.

But what was his situation? He was being detained, that was certain. This method of imprisonment was not regular in any sense. Where was all this going? When would there be a resolution? Was all this because of a lost file? Where was the Director? Was he likewise being held somewhere? Would there ultimately be confessions, trials, public vilification?

These thoughts were becoming unwelcome and tending towards ever greater darkness. Weiss got to his feet and paced the empty office like a caged animal. He set himself to walk a number of paces clockwise, carefully counting out the steps. Then he marched counter-clockwise for the same number of paces.

Not-Else appeared with a tray of food – bread, sausage, fruit. He was given a bottle of mineral water. Weiss noted that he was not to be provided with any cutlery. Tentatively he asked if he could have something to read. The request was ignored.

Weiss found that he was ravenous and attacked the food, plain as it was. The cleared plate was removed and Not-Else disappeared from the floor.

Again Weiss set about his pacing until he felt himself tired enough for sleep. He visited the washroom. He had decided that he must try to keep to some sort of schedule and habitual routine if he was to cling on to his sanity.

Was that it, he wondered? Was this all designed to finally drive him insane. Was the intention to drive him out of his wits and then incarcerate him in some state mental institution?

That was where this story about Lil leaving him had come from. This was just another element of the plot to rob him of his sanity. He had them there though. He could trust Lil. He could trust in Lil. He wouldn't let them break him. They'd find Ludovic Weiss a tough nut to crack.

Routine, that was what he needed. He brushed his teeth. He found pyjamas in the pile of his clothes. He changed and got under the blankets.

Thus between periods of wakefulness and speculation punctuated by the monotonous diet of bread, sausage and fruit and fitful sleep under the bright, white, unforgiving glare of the office lights time passed for Ludovic Weiss.

The noise of movement and talking from the outer office signalled to Weiss that the working week had started. Weiss was already dressed and he sat on the camp bed ready to face whoever might come through the office doorway.

Gerd and Mart between them carried a desk, an exact replica of Weiss' but obviously much newer, into the bare office space. Chairs, filing cabinets and the other paraphernalia of office work followed before Mart sat himself behind the desk. At no time did either man acknowledge Weiss' presence. If they glanced in his direction they looked straight through him as if he did not exist.

Not-Else brought in coffee and biscuits on a china plate. Gerd left and Mart settled down to work. To Weiss it was like watching a facsimile of his own past life as Mart fielded telephone calls, stared at a computer screen or shuffled the various papers that were handed across the desk.

Weiss tried to speak to Mart but he was ignored.

Others passed through the office. Some sat and engaged in discussion with Mart as he lounged behind the desk. Others stepped in briefly to exchange a word or two, a mixture of cryptic exchanges in office jargon or mild banter. Several times Not-Else reminded Mart that he had an appointment and he left the office abruptly, gathering a sheaf of papers only to return within the space of an hour.

Promptly at midday Gerd dropped by and the two of them went off to the staff restaurant.

Throughout all the proceedings which repeated themselves day on day, no-one paid the slightest attention to Weiss. No-one made eye contact with him or exchanged a word with him or about him. He moved among them like a ghost never touching any of them.

After the first rebuff from Mart, Weiss tried to talk with anyone else who passed into the office. There were many familiar faces but all of them failed to hear him or acknowledged him.

It felt to Weiss as if the real world had been surrounded by an impermeable glass wall and that he had been placed on the outside. The feeling of exclusion twisted at Weiss' mind and seemed to cause him actual physical pain as if he had received a sharp blow to the stomach.

Weiss's only form of communication was with Not-Else and that only when she brought his food or told him to do something specific such as when to wash, when to tidy his things. The food, though adequate for the support of life, was unchanging and uninteresting.

Weiss began to obsess about food with taste. He craved simple things. He remembered favourite foods with great and painful clarity. Jam, butter and eggs. He thirsted for a mug of tea or the cool, hoppy bite of beer at the back of his throat. The smell of coffee in the morning when Not-Else brought Mart his first mug of the day nearly drove Weiss mad.

He tried to draw her into a dialogue. He asked when the Director would come to see him. He asked for books, writing materials. He was ignored except when a curt refusal was offered.

At night on the first day of his exclusion from the living world, when everybody had left the office Weiss ventured to examine the new equipment and furniture that had been brought in. He sat behind the desk and experienced a cocktail of emotions, the top note of which was jealousy with an undertone of bitterness. His place had been usurped and by Mart of all people. He was being shown daily an image of what he once had been. It was the knife twisting in his vitals.

He tried the desk drawers and found them all to be locked. All files and other papers had been carefully locked away. He tried to turn on the computer on

Mart's desk but was met with a demand for a password. Naturally his own old passwords were rejected. He tried to guess the new ones, Mart's birthdate possibly or his dog's name. Eventually the account was locked and the computer turned itself off.

The next morning When Mart tried to use his computer he too was locked out and spent a good deal of time convincing the computer department to reinstate his account. For several nights after that Weiss performed the same service and sat watching the ensuing morning performance with something approaching mirth. Then the computer was locked away and that entertainment was denied him.

Weiss also tried all the telephones he could find. There was never a dial tone; they all seemed to shut off at a scheduled time of day. He would not be discouraged. Instead he sat listening to faint hiss on the line for minutes together in the hope of someone being on the other end.

Soon he started to talk to himself simply to hear the sound of his own voice and to elicit a response. He rationalised his behaviour by imagining someone locked away in a room somewhere in the building listening to him over the microphones he knew to be hidden in the walls.

"I know you're there, "he almost shouted. "I know you're listening. I'm not going mad. I'm just talking to you."

For hours he held the hidden listener in a very one-sided conversation. He asked questions which never drew a response.

"Are you married? Children? You have children? How did you get into a job like this? What did you study at university?"

And from the imagined responses he built himself a picture of the silent listener and his life.

So Weiss's phantom existence continued from day to day and days became weeks until he lost count of how long he had been held here.

That morning began like any other. It must have been a week day because there were people there. When Gerd arrived at the door he was a little breathless and his speech had something of the portentous about it.

"She's on her way."

Mart was cool and collected. "OK. No need to get excited. Will she want coffee do you think?"

"Don't expect so. You ready?"

"Yeah. I'm ready. Of course I'm ready. Been a long time coming."

Just then the Director swept into the office and took the visitor's chair in front of Mart's desk. Gerd looked about, saw the chair piled with Weiss' clothes and shot the garments on the floor. He placed the chair beside Mart's desk and sat so that he too was facing the Director. She didn't seem to be in too much of hurry to get down to business. She glanced around the office with approval. As with everybody else Weiss was or seemed to be invisible to her.

"You seem to have settled in here alright Mart. I hope Lil isn't too worn out after looking after us all yesterday."

"Not at all, we enjoyed having you."

"It's good to get together informally from time to time. Good for the department. Thank Lil for me again."

Weiss had not seen the Director since she had had him first brought here and into this bizarre form of captivity. Her appearance alone had excited his curiosity. Now mention of 'Lil' grabbed his attention. This couldn't be his Lil who was being spoken of? Lil with Mart? Impossible! Unthinkable! Devastating!

"You and Lil seem to be settling in nicely, Mart."

"Yes, we're very happy, thank you."

"She's certainly got the apartment looking very comfortable."

"Kind of you to say so."

This was a subtle torture that even Torquemada would have been proud to set his name to. Was this little scenario set up just to bring him to his knees or to finally drive him out of his mind? Weiss took a step towards the group, a word of protest or a squeal of anguish on his lips.

A figure entered the office. It was the grey man from the Intertrade offices. The man he had chased into the building. He is employed by the department? The Director turned to greet him.

"We've been waiting for you. Get a seat and join us. We haven't started.

The grey man ducked out of the office and returned with a chair. He sat by the Director. In their position they all offered their backs to Weiss, shutting him out. The director reached into her briefcase and brought out a slim red file that was all too familiar to Weiss. Frustration and anger compelled him to demand sharply:

"So you had it all along. Did you take it from the apartment? Where did you get it?"

Nobody in the group gathered around Mart's desk showed any reaction to his outburst. Weiss tried to thrust himself into the group but he was unseen. The Director continued calmly with what was obviously a briefing

"There's a summary. Top sheet."

"Answer me," Weiss demanded his voice rising to a screech.

Again no response. Weiss' instinct was to grab the Director or one of the group and shake the truth from them. He held himself back by a monumental effort of restraint.

Mart was handling the file, scanning the top sheet. He handed it on to Gerd who read and in turn passed it to the grey man.

"Damning stuff isn't it?" the Director continued. The others murmured their assent.

Weiss was squirming. This conversation almost precisely reflected his own talk with the other Director in the church. He yelled as much into the unhearing ears and uncomprehending faces of the quartet sat around the desk.

"This is the foundation of the case, of course. But you have each been working separately on aspects of the investigation. It's time to put all the findings together. I'm assuming you are all in a position to do that?"

The three men nodded, a ragged bobbing of heads. They agreed they were indeed ready

Weiss felt a sudden surge of relief. This sounded to him that a case was at last being put together. Maybe a prosecution, a trial was in the offing. The frustration of his exclusion had built to an exploding point. He lurched into the middle of the group and demanded at the top of his voice:

"Let me be part of this! I can help. Let me in. Let me in. Don't shut me out."

He sank to his knees as the quartet broke apart and retreated to the four corners of the room. He burst into tears, chest heaving, as the dam holding back his emotions crumbled and burst. Not-Else came briskly into the room and lifted him bodily onto the bed. She took up position between Weiss and the group who reformed about the desk and settled back to conversation as if no disturbance had interrupted their deliberations.

Weiss pulled the cover over his head blotting out the light but he still heard the Director finish the briefing and leave the room. The three men talked among themselves for a short time then the grey man took his leave.

"Better get on with it then." from Mart

"No rest for the wicked eh?"

"Quick one on the way home, eh. Lil's got a class tonight so no rush."

"Sure. Why not?"

Weiss stayed under the blanket for some time. Not-Else brought his tray and set it beside the bed. When he was sure that everyone had left for the night, Weiss sat up. He took the tray to the desk and ate his supper. Between mouthfuls he chatted to the unseen and unresponsive listener he knew to be there:

"I've no purpose. I've been stripped of everything. I wish for a cell you know. I was part of this. Now they make me watch but it's just my nose pressed up against the glass."

He finished the food and pushed the tray away from him. He picked up the phone and listened to the hiss on the line.

"Help me!" he croaked. "Help me!"

OPPORTUNITY?

Weiss was lying on the camp bed, his eyes closed, and his mind drifting, when he noticed the change. The hum of the air-conditioning was no longer there in the background of his hearing. It had been replaced by a featureless silence. He opened his eyes to semi-darkness. The stark white light from the fluorescent fittings was gone and only the dim glow of the emergency lighting feebly illuminated the office.

Weiss realised that the power had failed. He lay in the semi-darkness waiting for the building's standby power generators to start up and the lighting and air-conditioning to return to normal. At any moment he expected to hear the thud of the security team's boots as they checked out the building.

Nothing happened.

Weiss began to count off seconds in his head. When he reached six hundred he realised that the power was not coming back on. He was surprised that the security guards had not put in an appearance but then rationalised that the night-time skeleton staff were probably busy dealing with the emergency.

He swung his legs over the side of the bed and stood up. Weeks of inactivity had already robbed him of what little physical fitness he had had and at first he could only stand until the dizziness of vertigo cleared. His head on one side he listened to the stillness. No-one was coming.

Weiss, careful to make no noise in the overpowering silence of the dead building, walked on tiptoe to the door and opened it a crack. The outer office was also in gloom, lighted only by the dim emergency lighting. Weiss ventured through the door and into the outer corridor. Still no sign of life.

He walked the length of the corridor until he reached the security gate. Tentatively he reached out and gave the bars of the turnstile a poke with the tips of his fingers. It gave to his touch and clicked around to the next position. Emboldened by this small success but still not believing in this turn of fate, Weiss pushed hard on the turnstile and was elated when the gate revolved one complete turn in response. In his mind a vision of freedom began to form. It was there for the taking; he had only to seize it. Weiss hesitated.

Was this a trap? Another form of humiliation? Another ploy to crush his spirit? Weiss began to tremble and felt that his legs were on the point of crumpling beneath him. What he should do, he told himself, was crawl back under the rough blanket and shut all this from his mind. The power would come on at any minute. Unsure, he stood, rocking back and forward on his heels until, as if by accident, he pitched forward against the turnstile. The gate gave under his weight and Weiss felt himself tumbling through and landing on his knees as his trembling thighs gave way under him.

Weiss rested on all fours, listening. Still nothing, not a sound. The elevator door stood open, inviting him to climb inside. Weiss dragged himself to his feet and slumped into the lift, leaning against the metal walls, gathering his senses. It was several minutes before it dawned on him that the lift was going nowhere. The buttons on the control panel were dull and unilluminated. There was no power and he had wasted precious minutes. The power would be back on at any time. The security teams were working on it as he stood there.

Weiss lurched from the dead elevator car and threw himself through the swing doors that protected the stairwell. He descended the stairs as fast as his weakened legs would allow. At the first landing he stopped to listen, pressing himself into the rough concrete wall. Still there was no sign of anyone else. He descended two more floors and was forced to pause to catch his breath and ease the ache in his lungs. Just on the edge of his hearing he heard a door slam somewhere below him.

Weiss hugged the wall, trying to meld himself into the concrete. He stooped forward straining to hear any sound that might rise up to him. A beam from a torch climbed the void towards him, swept above his head and was gone. Again, beneath him, a door slammed. Then silence.

Slowly now Weiss inched his way down to the next level. He paused again, listening. How many more floors before he reached the ground? Possibly ten, he supplied the dispiriting answer.

Again the sound of doors and now a mumbled and indistinct conversation reached him from below. The security team were checking each stairwell in turn, Weiss reasoned. Would they be looking for him? Could they have noted his absence from his place of captivity already? At last Weiss' head cleared and he began to reason rationally. They couldn't know he had escaped the confines of the office floor yet. He had been gone just a few minutes and no-one had passed him on the stairs. So, the danger of discovery was below him.

The sound of doors slamming again reached him but now from further below. The guards were checking each floor but heading downwards. Weiss reasoned that all he had to do was stay at least one floor above the guards until he reached the ground floor. Listening carefully for sounds from beneath, he started to descend floor by floor, pausing at each landing until a further slamming of doors marked the downward progress of the search team. With each successive floor Weiss convinced himself that he was not the quarry in this case but that the security guards were following routine procedures.

Thus assured Weiss had descended to the penultimate landing before the ground floor when he heard very distinct voices and boots begin to ascend the staircase. If he tried to out climb the security guard in his condition he would soon be caught, the only chance was to hide out on this floor and hope that the guards would climb upward to check out the senior management floors. Silently Weiss opened the access door and slipped through. He held the door, preventing it from slamming closed and eased it into position. Hardly breathing he knelt behind the door and listened as in the next moment booted footsteps passed him and carried on upwards. Still kneeling Weiss waited and his patience was rewarded as yet more boots crunched up the stairs.

Weiss waited, still on his knees and counting off the seconds. When he was convinced that no more guards were following the group who had already climbed past him he got to his feet. It was now only a matter of a few minutes before his escape would be discovered. He would simply have to take a chance that no further security men were waiting for him at the ground floor exit. He launched himself through the door into the stairwell and ran down the stairs, plunging through fire door and into the cool night air and a small taste of freedom.

Weiss plunged into the enveloping darkness and jog stumbled across the empty parking area, anxious to put as much distance as possible between himself and the darkened building. He paused leaning on the wall of the empty and unlit gatekeepers' booth, to catch his breath which was coming in painful rasps. The vehicle gates had failed in the downward position but the pedestrian gate swung invitingly open. Weiss passed through and stood in the empty street.

Now that he had a moment to consider the hopeless nature of his position dawned upon him. All he had were the clothes he stood up in, shirt, trousers and shoes. He had no money and no identification papers. The first police patrol that he encountered would take him off the streets and to a cell without a second thought. He needed to find a place to hide out, someone to help him. He thought of Lil and the apartment, knowing that that was never going to be a solution. Lil was with someone else and the apartment was no longer a place of safety. He needed to put distance between himself and the building. Maybe he should leave the city.

Looking around him Weiss saw that some of the other office blocks had a sprinkling of lights on some of their floors. Beyond the immediate area that surrounded the Compliance Department building the street lights were still lit. It appeared that the power failure had only affected the Department headquarters.

He had no idea of the time or even what day it was. Judging by the lack of traffic business hours were long past. It might have been the weekend or late on a week night. He began to walk away from the building, not even conscious of the direction he was taking.

He saw a car approaching. Its headlights punched through the darkness as it came towards him. For a moment he considered flagging the motorist down and placing himself at their mercy. Then he drew back and hunched himself into the darkness. The car sped on by.

Panic seized him. He had to get off the streets. If he stayed out here it would only be a matter of time before he was taken. He plunged on into the night, head down and shivering in the chill air. He rounded a corner and a blaze of neon confronted him. It was the brightly lit frontage of The Annex, the familiar watering hole of happier times. Was this the refuge he was seeking? Or was this a trap? He realised that after all this time he had no knowledge of what waited for him on the other side of the bar's plate glass door.

Desperation drove his footsteps. He reached the door and plunged through it without pausing to consider. He stood swaying on the threshold as the door swished gently closed behind him. He looked around. Two men in shirtsleeves, beer bellies swelling over their belts were using the dart board. The click of billiard balls sounded in his ears. He turned and saw a group gathered around the pool table. A woman in a bright dress sat at the bar.

"What the…Ludo? Is that you Ludo?" came from behind the bar.

Weiss focussed and saw the familiar form of Lex the barman.

"You look awful. What's happened?" Already the barman had come from behind the counter and reached Weiss just in time to catch him as his knees buckled.

Weiss had not thought through what would happen when he entered The Annex. What came out of his mouth was pure inspiration.

"Mugged. I've been mugged."

"When…where?"

"Just now. Around the corner. I was leaving the office…"

"I'll get the police."

The last thing that Weiss wanted. He dragged himself upright using Lex as a prop.

"No…no police. Just let me sit down."

"But they might still be around…the muggers. How many?"

The woman had climbed down from her bar stool and now had an arm around Weiss.

"Let him sit. You know the police won't get here for ages and then all they do is ask pointless questions."

Between them Lex and the woman got Weiss to a seat in a booth. The barman waved the woman away and she went back to her seat.

"Sit tight Ludo, I'll get you something."

"I've got no money...they took it. And my papers."

"Sure, sure. Don't worry I'll sort you out."

Lex was back directly and placed a glass of brandy in front of Weiss. He gestured to Weiss that he should drink. Weiss took down the fiery liquid in a single gulp. Lex brought another glass.

"Where've you been Ludo? You haven't been in for months."

"Away," Weiss improvised. "I've been on an assignment. Just got back."

"Ah. I thought you'd abandoned us. And you get mugged as soon as you get back home. Tough break I call that."

Weiss was thinking furiously. Maybe he could touch Lex for a loan; enough to get him away from the city. Maybe he could borrow a coat. It was Lex who took the initiative.

"So, you don't want me to call the police?"

"No...they won't do anything. And there'll be questions."

"I get you. I guess you'll need some cash."

"That would help. I can get a taxi. Home. You haven't got a spare coat I can borrow? It's pretty cold out there."

"Sure. I'll fix you up. You still living at the same place? I'm closing up soon. I can give you a ride."

Weiss had to think fast. This was too much too soon.

"That's good of you. But no…I've moved. Quite far out…I couldn't ask…"

"What are friends for? I'll take you. Where exactly."

Again Weiss answered without thinking, naming the district where all his problems had started. He could get Lex to drop him by the derelict church and disappear into the streets around there. The barman told Weiss to just relax, get himself together. He'd just go upstairs and get an old coat he had up there.

Weiss sipped at the warming brandy and felt relief creep through him. He closed his eyes and allowed himself to think beyond the immediate. He began to form a plan of escape.

Lex returned with a black overcoat that smelled of stale beer and dust. He dumped it beside Weiss and placed another glass on the table. He took the empty glass from Weiss telling him that he would close up in a few minutes then they'd be off.

Weiss waited. He was calmer now. His head drooped on his chest. He could barely keep his eyes open. He forced himself awake but the struggle proved too difficult. He drifted into the darkness of sleep.

A heavy hand on his shoulder shook him awake. At first he couldn't remember where he was. Then the memory flooded back. He looked up. Mart was looming above him. Across the table Gerd was sitting, a half-empty beer glass in front of him.

"Just like old times eh, Ludo? Time to go home now!"

Weiss felt himself yanked roughly to his feet and dragged from the booth. Gerd left his seat and took his other arm. Lex was out of sight as he was propelled through the glass door and into the cold night air.

TIME STOPS

Weiss withdrew into himself. He avoided contact with the office staff who continued to carry out their duties around him by confining himself to his bed. He lay under the covers, peeping out to observe the activities that went on. At night, which he presumed to be signalled by the mass migration from the offices, or at weekends when no-one came, he left his nest and haunted the empty corridors.

Occasionally a newspaper or ancient magazine was left in a waste basket or on a desk. He seized on these eagerly as a means of diverting his mind from the continual speculations that ran in his head. Why was he being held? Why had Lil betrayed him? What crime had he committed? When, if ever, would this situation be ended? These questions and their possible answers spun through his mind in maddening spirals that never resolved but instead looped back on themselves.

He scoured each article of news for information about the Director and about Intertrade. Had the Director been arrested? Was there a trial? A significant figure like the Director surely couldn't simply be made to disappear? And Intertrade? Had the scandal erupted? Had there been arrests? Nothing was reported.

As for himself, he was unsurprised that there had been no notice of his disappearance in any of the newspapers he managed to see. Who might have noted his absence from everyday life? He realised with bitterness that his footprint on the planet was without significance.

With the rest of the reading matter he managed to glean he rationed himself strictly, a few paragraphs or a page a day. He noted articles that seemed of especial interest and read and reread them several times. One day he turned a page and saw a picture of a smiling bride and groom. The happy couple were Lil and Mart. There was no mistake, the text beneath confirmed it. So it had been true, just as he had overheard. Lil and Mart. He turned the page and wept silently.

As time passed the frustration and monotony of his imprisonment began to tell on Weiss. He needed distraction. The fragments of newspapers that were left around were not enough to distract him. He determined to write out his own version of events. Maybe it could be smuggled to the outside. There was still a free press. Maybe the story would get picked up and enquiries made.

There was plenty of blank paper around the offices. He took several sheets from the pile by the printer in the outer office. He needed something to write with and that was more of a problem. He searched the offices and corridors for several days and could find nothing. Then he came upon a stub of pencil that had been discarded in a waste bin and not removed. The point was blunted and there was only about two inches of wood left but it would do. He hid it and the paper in his pile of clothes.

For several days he put off starting to write down his narrative. He thought of the papers and the pencil hidden within the pile of clothing with warmth. They represented a new salvation and he was anxious not to waste the opportunity by a false start. He lay on the bed staring at the ceiling composing and savouring cogent phrases which he would fit into the story. Then he felt himself ready and compelled to action.

Each night, for several nights he worked steadily recording the events that had occurred and his speculations on the truths that seemed shrouded in these mysteries. When the pencil was blunted he hunted around for a knife or sharpener. Eventually he resorted to the rough edge at the rear of the filing cabinet. It was not very efficient, he must have spent hours carefully working the point anxious not to waste any of the precious graphite.

When he was forced to break off he carefully concealed the written document beneath the mattress on which he slept. Eventually he had managed to cover four sheets of the typing paper. When he read it over it seemed even to him who had lived these scenes a crazy invention. Was it a madman who had held the pencil?

He knew it all to be the truth and maybe there was someone else out there who might believe his story.

Now he was faced with the question of how to get his document to the world. Maybe he could bribe Not-Else. He laughed out loud at the thought. How and with what? Then who else was there. He was effectively being held in isolation. He decided to sleep on the matter and slipped the papers under the thin mattress.

He had not managed to come up with a solution to his problem when several days later Not-Else decided that he should take a shower. When he returned he looked for his clothes. They had all been removed and in their place he found a coarse grey gown, like a night-shirt. Not-Else told him to put it on and ignored his query as to the whereabouts of his own clothes. As she was leaving him Not-Else turned and produced the sheaf of papers that he had hidden.

"I found these, by the way. In case you miss them."

It was no surprise to Weiss that the Director came to see him the next evening when everybody else had left the building. He had just finished his evening meal and was sitting behind the desk when she came in and took a seat across from him. She sat and looked him over, then:

"What's this? You are letting yourself go. You look like you are wearing a shroud."

"She took my clothes."

"Who?"

"Her. That woman."

"Else. You mean Else?"

"She is not Else."

"Still obdurate then? You persist with your illusions? I told you, acceptance is the only way."

"Why have I deserved this?

"You are right to blame yourself."

"Is this all about that damned file?"

"Possibly."

"Or the assignment?"

"Both...possibly."

"Yes?"

"Or possibly not at all."

"Is this about the other Director? My Director. Do you think I am loyal to him? You replaced him. You see me as a threat?"

"Are you loyal?"

"To you?"

"Loyalty is to be admired."

"I'd be loyal to you."

"But it can also be misguided. Misplaced. You ought to think carefully before you trust someone with your loyalty."

"I'd work for you."

"There is no work for you."

"There's nothing here for me?"

"You exist, here."

The director sat back and sighed. She produced the sheets of paper that Weiss had last seen in not-Else's hand.

"You do disappoint me Weiss. What is this all about?"

"I want release."

"Ah, there's the dilemma.

"I need release."

"That's a dilemma, right there, a dilemma. Or is it a paradox? What do you think?"

The Director stood and paced. She went over to the bed and pulled back the covers. She returned to Weiss and stood to one side of him, "You're not a prisoner, you see. Words like release and sentence have no meaning for you, for your condition."

"But what is this if it isn't a prison?"

"Maybe it's for your own protection. Maybe we are keeping you safe. Had you thought of that?"

"That's not how it feels."

"I think you are making your own cage."

"No. That's not right."

"All you have to do is accept. Then you'll be happy."

"Release me. Then I'll be happy."

"Weiss listen to me, this is not the way to secure a release, "and the Director tossed the hand written sheets onto the desk. "This is not a sign of cooperation. How could we trust you, trust in you, if you act in this underhand way?"

Weiss waited for the Director to continue. There seemed nothing further to be said.

"Who did you expect to believe this? It reads like the ravings of madman or possibly a fabulist. Is that it? Are you trying to convince us that you have lost your wits?"

"Wouldn't that be satisfactory to you? Isn't this what all these mind games are about?"

"And how did you expect to get these writings outside of this building?"

"I hadn't thought that through," Weiss admitted a little shamefaced.

"So you were going to hide this and deceive us until you found a way. When we let something slip. Like the stub of pencil someone carelessly left around."

The Director looked at Weiss for some time in silence. Eventually she seemed to have resolved a difficult decision. There was regret in her voice as she spoke.

"Very well Weiss. I'd hoped that you would take my advice and just accept what has to happen to you. You are becoming a problem and it's of your own making. Why do you insist on being so obdurate?"

"Because it's my right. I want to know why you are doing this to me. What have I done? Why am I being kept here? What really happened?"

"You don't appreciate the consequences of what you ask. But alright. I suppose we need to get to a conclusion. How long have you been with the Department?"

Despite his irritation Weiss sensed that he might at last be on the verge of achieving some understanding. He tried to answer as calmly as possible but could not resist adding a barb.

"Five years. But you know this already. It appears you know things about me even I don't know."

"You can at least treat me with some respect Weiss. Just work with me and you'll get what you think you want. Remember who is in control here. Now who recruited you?"

"The Director. Not you, the other one."

"Yes, yes. We are clear on that. He came to the university. He singled you out. I expect you felt quite flattered by that."

"I was actually. It's nice when your qualities are recognised."

"He recognised your qualities alright. You were just what he was looking for. He groomed you."

"Groomed me? I suppose he did. Nothing wrong in that. I prefer to think that he mentored me."

"The rapid promotions must have given you pause for thought? Did you ever wonder what might be behind your meteoric rise from the ranks?"

Weiss shook his head. Where was all this going?

"You probably put it down to your own talent and capacity for delivering results. You're quite egotistical you know, Weiss. Luckily your rise was noted by others, others who did ask questions. At the same time the Director's behaviour was also falling under scrutiny. Do you understand what I am saying?"

So his champion, the man who had elevated him to the superior position he enjoyed, had been the subject of enquiries even as he was recruiting Weiss? This was starting to feel unpleasant. Weiss felt himself under attack. He couldn't go back now. The director was continuing.

"You see what the Director saw in you was a fall-guy. Someone he could use as a human shield if his machinations were uncovered. He saw a malleable character, a weak character. He saw a man of no significance that he could mould and control and eventually sacrifice for his own preservation."

"So the assignment...?"

"...Was designed to set you up. And of course to get him off the hook. He had figured out that he was under suspicion and that evidence had been accruing. This place is like a sieve when it comes to leaks and rumours. You've found that out yourself. It's true that the only secret is one that only one person knows about. If I tell you my secret then it's not a secret any longer. That's why I always smile to myself when someone goes on about a suspected conspiracy.

Anything covert leaks out eventually. And it doesn't take long. Shall I go on?"

Weiss nodded agreement. This was very unpleasant but he had to know and understand.

"The whole story with Intertrade was a sham. He was going to use you to plant false evidence against them and shift the blame for his own crimes onto them. He was desperate by then and the plan such as it was does have a hint of madness about it."

"And what about me? What if the plan failed?"

"You'd have been left holding the baby! When everyone else had left the room you would have been the only one left in the spotlight. You only have to look at where you have finished up to test the validity of that assertion."

"And what were you doing there? That day of the meeting with the Intertrade people?"

"It was an intervention. We knew what his plan was. The people in that room knew all about it."

"But how…."

"Did he know what you would do? He knew exactly what you would do. He had groomed you, remember. You're his creation!"

So his whole career had been a construct to cover for the Director. All the success, all the plaudits merely preparation for his sacrifice. When had all this started? Had he been pointed out as a likely patsy or had the Director sensed in him the necessary character faults that could be used. Had there been some professor who disliked him? What about earlier...schooldays, youth organisations, field trips? Who and when? All of it a personal conspiracy that lead inevitably to this point.

Weiss had been happy teaching at the university. Nevertheless the glittering future held out to him by the Director had tempted him. That must have been it. The Director had been tipped off by one of Weiss' jealous colleagues. That had always been a danger. That was one that had followed him here. Yes Mart and Gerd; there were two prime examples.

As if sensing his thoughts the Director remarked:

"Come now Weiss. You are not some tragic hero. You're just a man who was used. It happens all the time."

It was an unlooked for note of humanity. She continued:

"I suppose you want to know what's become of him. Well, you must have guessed that we have secured him. We took him that night when you put in your unwelcome appearance at his house."

"Why were you there? When I showed, I mean," Weiss wanted to know.

"We knew you'd make for his house. In fact we gave you all the encouragement that was needed to make it happen. I was there to make sure you didn't get in our way and somehow foul up our arrangements."

144

He'd been played in every sense. Weiss squirmed inside and felt himself shrink within his skin.

"There won't be a trial. We've committed him to a secure asylum. We couldn't risk this getting out in public, laying the facts before them. That would be too harmful to the department. Effectively we've made him disappear."

"And what about me?"

"Weiss you are a man of no significance but you are a loose end. Loose ends get pulled." And she waved Weiss's document under his nose. "This is such a thread. I don't know what you were thinking but this is your own fault"

Weiss sat in silence. When she spoke the Director's voice held just a hint of humane compassion:

"I told you, acceptance was all that was needed. But you would insist on knowing and you've become troublesome. You've given us a problem. A few more weeks, maybe months, some rehabilitation and who knows? Too late now though. I expect we'll work out what to do eventually. Here, you might like this."

She handed Weiss a book. It was a small gesture of humanity. Weiss turned it over and read the title, "Conspiracies across the Centuries."

The director stood and walked to the door. She turned back for a parting word:

"I'm sorry it has to end like this for you but you can see we have no other choice. You are guilty of nothing except trusting in the wrong people. Our American friends call it collateral damage. That's you I'm afraid – collateral damage."

Weiss sat behind the desk hearing the Director's footsteps receding down the hallway. So, now he knew the truth and it was a bitter truth. His whole picture of himself had been tarnished forever. He had been played for a fool over all these years. Now he had been robbed of everything that he valued.

THE END OF TIME

After his last interview with the Director Weiss fell into a decline. The Director's revelations had swept away the last element that connected him to humanity. He had been stripped of the ornaments of his identity, pushed out from the tribe and now his very faith had been taken from him.

What the Director had told him had furnished some sort of explanation for the madness that had overturned his comfortable life but at a huge cost. What did any explanation signify against a loss of faith? There was no-one left who he could believe in. He had been betrayed by his god figure. The other deities in his world had been stripped from him. Without some article of faith everything else was meaningless. Nothing mattered to Weiss.

Weiss no longer pondered on what had happened to him. He no longer tried to make sense of his situation or to try to understand the motives for his treatment. He did not think of his losses or try to fathom the loss of his wife, his family or his friendships. He no longer hoped for release of any kind. He became inert.

For hours he lay on the camp bed merely staring at the wall until his eyes hurt. Then he slept. He must have dreamed but on waking he remembered nothing.

Not-Else continued to bring him food and drink. At first he continued to eat what was placed in front of him but gradually he ignored the offerings of bread and sausage and fruit. He drank little, just enough to relieve the dryness of lips and throat.

The life of the office continued around him unabated. The daily rhythms played out without pause. Mart continued to occupy the desk and to conduct whatever business he was engaged in. Visitors for Mart came and went. Gerd dropped by punctually at meal times and the pair left for the restaurant together. The grey man came by for meetings. The sound of Not-Else typing, filing, phoning came from the outer office. Weiss ignored all of this and turned his face to the wall.

Likewise the inhabitants of the office world, the world of working and striving people, ignored Weiss. Apart from when Not-else delivered his food nobody paid him any attention and avoided the tiny patch of territory which he now occupied.

When, like the tide ebbing, the office emptied at the end of the working day and he had the place to himself, Weiss no longer wandered the corridors or paced his own cell. He didn't sit behind the desk, as before, and try to recall his days of power and prestige. When documents or newspapers were, by an oversight, left out, he simply ignored them. They held no potential interest for him.

He neglected his own personal hygiene. He went unshaven and left his hair which had grown to an unruly length, in a wild and unwashed tangle. From time to time Not-Else told him that he stank and ordered him under the shower. Naked in the wash room he turned away from the image of a sub-human that presented itself to him in the mirror.

Likewise Not-Else enforced a change of clothing on the compliant Weiss at regular intervals, laying a laundered version of the coarse grey garment on the bed while Weiss made use of the shower.

He became weaker, spending more and more time laying on his bed while the world continued about him. He fixed his attention on the ceiling and became familiar with the small fissures and cracks in the plaster work. He noticed, without emotion or interest, a small spider weave a web in the corner. With similar lack of engagement he saw the web disintegrate and the spider, undaunted recommence construction.

As his strength, physical and mental, deteriorated he experienced hallucinations. Lil stood beside the bed, looking down at him. For a moment he felt some desire to know what had motivated her to leave him pass through his mind. It faded as soon as it came and he turned away to the wall. He was glad that when he turned back the ghost of his wife had left him.

Likewise the Director, that is the Director who had so ill-used him, visited him in phantom and illusory form.

Weiss found that he had nothing to say, no question to ask of the ghostly apparition.

He must have been sleeping deeply because he had not been aware of the forms gathering around him. At first he thought they were probably visitants conjured by old memory but then he heard their talk.

There was mention of his condition. A suggestion that now was a time for a doctor to be called. He heard the Director agree and give orders. Weiss drifted away again.

Later still he was woken up by movement near him. Mart and Gerd were carrying a large object between them. They set it down and left the office. They did not look at the Weiss where he lay.

The coffin lay on the floor beside Weiss's bed exactly in his eye line. The black ebony shone sumptuously in the hard artificial light. It was with consummate satisfaction that Weiss noted the gilded handles. It seemed to call to him.

Weiss tried to stand but his legs had atrophied to a point where they could no longer sustain him unaided. He sank to his knees and crawled to the coffin. He peered inside and was gratified to see the pristine white of the satin lining like a bed of snow. There was even a pillow for his head.

At last, here was something appropriate to his status. He ran his hand over the smooth wood at the lip of the coffin enjoying the sensation. He smelt the newness of the materials. He had contributed and now that contribution was being recognised.

Weiss levered himself into a kneeling position and bent into the coffin. It took no effort at all to roll himself into its welcoming embrace. He stretched himself out on the lining and positioned his head on the pillow. It just felt so right. It was like a homecoming.

The lid of the coffin had been propped against its opposite side. Weiss reached up and pulled at it. It must have been precisely positioned and balanced as it fell easily onto the top of the coffin, sealing the box exactly. For the first time in an age Weiss experienced the comfort of complete darkness.

He crossed his arms over his chest and enjoyed the sensation of complete isolation. There was no-one watching any more. He thought he could hear people outside. He distinctly heard screws being tapped home.

Ludovic Weiss lay back and closed his eyes and at last found peace.

Printed in Poland
by Amazon Fulfillment
Poland Sp. z o.o., Wrocław